The Time between Places

The Time Between Places

Stories That Weave In and Out
of Egypt and America

PAULINE KALDAS

The University of Arkansas Press
Fayetteville
2010

Manufactured in the United States of America

ISBN-10: (cloth) 1-55728-946-8
ISBN-13: (cloth) 978-1-55728-946-9

ISBN-10: (paper) 1-55728-945-X
ISBN-13: (paper) 978-1-55728-945-2

14 13 12 11 10 5 4 3 2 1

Designed by Liz Lester

♾ The paper used in this publication meets the minimum requirements of the American National Standard for Permanence of Paper for Printed Library Materials Z39.48-1984.

LIBRARY OF CONGRESS CATALOGING-IN-PUBLICATION DATA

Kaldas, Pauline, 1961–
The time between places : stories that weave in and out of Egypt and America / Pauline Kaldas.
p. cm.
ISBN 978-1-55728-947-6 (cloth : alk. paper) —
ISBN 978-1-55728-924-7 (pbk. : alk. paper)
1. Emmigration and immigration—Fiction. 2. Egyptians—United States—Fiction. 3. Americans—Egypt—Fiction. I. Title.
PS3611.A4326T56 2010

2010030212

*f*or my grandmother
who told me the first stories

and to my *f*amily
for all the stories we have shared

Contents

The Silence of Memory

Preface

This collection of stories traces the lives of different characters, all of whom are in some way inside the experience of emigrating from Egypt to the United States. It is the notion of time that anchors these stories. Yet it is also time that threatens to unravel these characters' lives as immigration moves them further away from the source of their identity and their place in the world. These characters are tangled in the vines of their history and culture, and it is impossible for them to release themselves. As a writer, it is the manner in which they are tangled that holds my interest.

The book is divided into four parts that are marked by phone calls across distance and time differences between a mother and a daughter. The process of separating from family and homeland stretches across the progression of these stories. The characters in the first part are located in Egypt, hovering around the desire and the possibility of emigration. The stories in the second part reveal characters that have recently immigrated and are in the process of creating new lives. The third group of stories traces characters that have been in America for a longer period and delves into their dreams of a homeland. The last set of stories opens the lives of the next generation as they negotiate the paths between their two worlds. The twenty stories in *The Time between Places* weave in and out of Egypt and America, revealing the tensions experienced by characters that are struggling with the cultural, political, and geographical boundaries of their lives.

Acknowledgments

Special thanks to all those who helped with this book: T. J. Anderson III, Yasmine Aida Anderson, Celine Aziza Kaldas Anderson, Marcia Douglas, Lisa Suhair Majaj, Khaled Mattawa, and Gayle Whittier. Their suggestions and encouragement made it possible for me to write these stories.

I am especially indebted to Alyssa Antonelli and Courtney Flerlage who read this manuscript with great care and offered their insights and recommendations.

Additional thanks to Larry Malley at the University of Arkansas Press, who responded to this manuscript with enthusiasm and believed in its publication.

My deep appreciation to Judith Ortiz Cofer for her essay, "5:00 A.M.: Writing as Ritual," which gave me a way to continue writing.

I am also grateful for the fellowship from the Virginia Commission for the Arts and the research grants I received from Hollins University that enabled me to work on this project.

"Airport" and "Bluebird" were originally published in *Dinarzad's Children: An Anthology of Contemporary Arab American Fiction,"* University of Arkansas Press, 2004.

"Cumin and Coriander," was originally published in *Ripe Guava,* 3 (2000).

"The Dancer" was originally published in *Mizna: Prose, Poetry, and Art Exploring Arab America,* 9.2 (2008).

"A Game of Chance" was originally published in *Callaloo* 32.4 (2010).

"He Had Dreamed of Returning" was originally published in *Dinarzad's Children: An Anthology of Contemporary Arab American Fiction,"* Second Edition, University of Arkansas Press, 2009.

"Suitors" was originally published in *Mizna: Prose, Poetry, and Art Exploring Arab America,* 5.2 (2003).

The Time between Places

Dream

I dreamt a strange dream—we were at the sea in Eskendria—and we entered the water—you were holding my hand—and the waves were high—and around us were children playing and happy—I was afraid of the waves—and you said to me don't be afraid mama, I'm holding your hand—and we kept going deeper into the water—and then you let go of my hand and you kept going in—and I kept calling you but you didn't hear me—and I was afraid to follow you—and the time passed—and the distance grew—until you were very far away—and you reached the other side—and barely I could see you like a dot on the horizon—and I couldn't reach you.

Chance Departures

Phone Call One

Aloo—Aloo—mama—*Aloo—ezayek ya mama* how are you mama—yes, we're well—*kol sana we entee tayeba* Merry Christmas—yes yes, we are all well—*ezay baba* how is dad—how is his health—and is my sister well, is she studying hard in college—yes, my daughter is fine and she is in a good school—and is my uncle well—tell him to stop smoking and drinking because of his diabetes—*kol sana we entoo tayebeen* Merry Christmas to all of you—yes, here they celebrate on December 25 but we are celebrating today with you—we will eat *mahshee* stuffed grape leaves—yes, we found grapeleaves but they are in a jar—there is no *molekhia*—I miss you mama—I wish we could be with you today—and are you well mama—what time is it over there—seven hours difference—here it is six in the morning—we got up early to call you—before the lines got busy—I miss you mama—*ma elsalama—ma elsalama*

A Game of Chance

Mustafa's hands worked deftly, his palms flipping the wrapped package over as his fingers intertwined the string to create a series of crisscross patterns that circled around the package and culminated in a tight bow at the center. He handed the package to the customer with a trained smile and received his tip with a magician's sleight of hand.

It was Thursday evening about nine o'clock, and the pastry store was lit up and crowded. Out of the corner of his eye, Mustafa could see two young women wearing headscarves, eating gelato. They were chatting and giggling, their faces animated with some secret joy. He would've liked to eavesdrop on their conversation, but the noise in the shop was too loud. An older woman with two young children was trying to place an order with one of the clerks as her children tugged at her dress, pointing to the chocolate cream puffs and strawberry tarts. The woman was requesting a tray of assorted *baklawa, kanafa,* and *basboosa,* the traditional Egyptian honey-soaked sweets. She finished placing her order and went to pay the cashier. As Mustafa wrapped her package, he watched her negotiate with the insistent children whose desire had led to tears and the threat of screams. With a heavy breath, he saw her surrender and buy a miniature éclair for each of them. As he handed her the package of pastries, the wrapping carefully tucked around it and held only by the elaborate design of strings, he knew his tip would be smaller because of her reluctant last purchase.

The two young women finished their gelato and followed the mother and children out of the store. Mustafa could hear the volume of noise decrease in the shop. Only a few men were left, most of them sent by their wives with orders to pick up sweets for the next day, Friday, the one guaranteed holiday each week. The day off seemed to relieve people from the necessary frugality of their lives, so business always picked up on Thursday. The male customers were the easiest. Usually they ordered a single tray of one kind of pastry: the round *kanafa* made of shredded wheat filled with either sweet cream or a mixture of nuts, the squares of *basboosa* made with semolina so its texture soaked with honey dissolved in the mouth, or the standard *baklawa* that was often shaped into small bird's nests stuffed with pistachios.

Mustafa took each cardboard tray of delicate sweets, and with a quick turn and twist, he wrapped the glossy paper over and under, tightening it with a repeated pattern of strings till it held its inner prize securely. Like a master chef who flips dough into the air and catches it effortlessly as it free-falls from the sky, Mustafa's movements were hypnotizing. The package seemed to be doing somersaults of its own free will. It was impossible to follow his exact actions, to know where he folded the paper or how he twined the string into an even pattern over it. His packages always held tight, whether the customer carried them by the knotted string in the middle or like a platter from the bottom; even if they were tilted in the carrying, the sweets would emerge whole and centered.

The men were consistent with their tips, usually fifty piasters, respectable but not generous. It was the women who were more erratic. The one with the two children gave him only twenty-five piasters. The wealthier Egyptian women usually gave him one pound. The foreigners were inconsistent too. They always seemed nervous, ill at ease, looking over their shoulders. The ones who could speak a little Arabic were often stingier than the others, giving him no more than fifty piasters. But the ones who were clearly tourists took out a wad of bills, unaccustomed to the art of tipping discreetly. They gave him as much as three or four pounds, handing him one pound at a time, unsure of when to stop, trying to calculate the equivalent in dollars. The foreigners always bought the Egyptian sweets, their eyes growing wide as they surveyed the shelves. They wanted to know what each item was called and what it was made of; in the end they bought a little of everything, hesitant to give up anything that might give them the taste they were craving.

There was one woman who came in often, sometimes as much as two or three times a week. She was Egyptian but had lived in America most of her life. Usually, she came in with her two daughters. She always went straight to the Egyptian sweets, but her daughters ran to the French pastries. She would look over at the girls, but he could see her eyes wandering to the *mille-feuilles* and the fruit tarts. Eventually the older daughter would gravitate to the Egyptian sweets and stand next to her mother. Together they would pick something out then return to the French pastries and the younger girl, inevitably to buy something else. She let her daughters choose what they liked, bought them whatever captured their fancy each time. She always gave him a two-pound tip, and he could see that she also tipped the man who got the pastries for her. She was friendly and more inclined to talk, not skittish like the foreigners and not frantic or tired like the Egyptians. From her conversations with the other workers, he had learned that she had lived in America most of her life. One day, he ventured a few words.

"America is nice," he said as he wrapped her packages a little slower than usual.

"Yes, it is," she said, "but Egypt is nice too."

"I'd like to go to America," he responded as if repeating a litany he had memorized.

Her smile flickered as she said, "Life is hard in America."

She picked up her packages, slipped the tip into his hand, and left with her children.

How could life be hard in America, he thought, when she can come in here and buy what she wants, satisfy her children's every desire? His one son was seven years old. When he was born, Mustafa named him Malek, meaning King. His wife had looked at him uncertainly when he had suggested the name. "That's a big name," she said. But he insisted; his son would do great things. Now it seemed to have been only a futile gesture. His son was just another ragged boy, growing up with a thin roof over his head and barely enough to eat. His wife was right: the poor should not aspire to greatness.

Mustafa wiped the sweat from his forehead and recalled his own aspirations. As a young boy, he used to hang around building sites, watching as men lifted and climbed, putting stone and steel together, the building rising as if the sky were pulling it up. Once, a manager asked him to hand some tools to one of the workers, and he rushed over imbued with the importance of his task. The manager gave him ten piasters, and Mustafa closed his fingers over it, feeling its cold metal against the sweat of his palm. When the building was completed, he looked up at it with pride, knowing he had made some contribution to its existence.

He dreamed of making these buildings, of creating something grand. When his last year of high school arrived and the *thanawiya amma* test loomed ahead, he studied, poring over books that blurred into the darkness of the night. His marks on the test would determine whether or not he would go to college and what subject he would be allowed to study. The engineering school required high grades that year. They had admitted too many students the previous year, so the admission grade was raised. When the day of the test arrived, he sat among thousands of students in the July heat, the words and numbers in front of him scrambling till he felt like he was doing a crossword puzzle where the spaces and the words were mismatched.

His scores were too low to admit him to college, and the disappointment entered him as if he'd swallowed a stone that had lodged in his organs. He wanted to repeat the last year of high school, so he could take the exam again, test his fate one more time. But his father refused. He needed to get a job, help the family, and support his younger brothers and sisters. Besides, his father argued, if his grade could not even admit him to college, how could he hope to get marks high enough for engineering? It was a fool's dream, his father said.

Mustafa swallowed his ambitions and began to work odd jobs wherever he could get them: at a mechanic shop, in a fruit stall, delivering groceries. He was always the one being given orders. Over time he learned that the best money came from tips, so he cultivated a smile, an easy manner that made people more willing to slip piasters into his palm.

One Friday, after prayers and the midday meal, his father sat with him as his mother served the dark coffee with a layer of foam brimming at the top. After setting the cups down, she slipped out of the room. His father cleared his throat and announced that Mustafa, now that he was twenty-five years old, was ready to get married. Mustafa felt his intestines twist and knot, his body held captive. The "Who?" from his lips sounded only like a slight release of breath.

"Your cousin, Mariam," declared his father, "is a good girl, my sister's daughter, well brought up, and now she's eighteen."

His father noticed the smoke of panic in his son's eyes.

"Don't worry," he said, "she's very pretty. You won't be disappointed."

The conversation ended as his father rose to take his afternoon nap. But he turned to Mustafa one more time.

"Your uncle knows someone at the pastry store on Kasr el Aini Street. He thinks he can get you a job there. You'll need more steady work."

Mustafa sat, the demitasse of coffee on the table in front of him still full, but the foam had now dissipated into murky liquid. He tried to focus his thoughts. When was the last time he saw Mariam? Her father visited often, but he could not recall Mariam or her mother. His mind struggled, placing images next to each other. When he finished high school, his uncle came over with his family to congratulate him. Mariam must've been around eleven, the scarf over her hair still new. She had tugged at it self-consciously. He remembered her large brown eyes and her wide mouth; her skin was smooth, and there was a softness to her round face. She had smiled shyly at him, and it relieved a little of the tension he was feeling at the time.

The thoughts swirled in Mustafa's mind. He could not imagine himself married. Where would they live? How would he take care of her? But in the days that followed, decisions were made for him, and he became only a spectator as his life was reshaped by others. He and Mariam were married; nothing more than his signature was expected. They moved into a small apartment not far from either of their parents in Sayyida Zeinab, surrounded by the same clutter of shops and narrow streets in which he had grown up.

He and Mariam had little opportunity to speak to one another before their wedding. Whenever they looked at each other, they seemed a bit alarmed, like the other person had suddenly appeared out of thin air. The courtship that followed their marriage was hesitant. Slowly, they grew accustomed to each other. But even years later, one of them would look up, surprised to see the other person as if having forgotten their presence.

Mustafa began work at the pastry shop on Kasr el Aini Street, walking through the Sayyida Zeinab alleyways, past the Metro station, and across the street where the shop bordered Garden City, an old neighborhood where some of the wealthier Egyptians lived. He started off sweeping the floor and wiping the glass cases to a sparkling shine, until one day the man who wrapped the packages didn't show up. He was asked to help out, and the manager gave him a brief explanation. As Mustafa started, he found that the job was almost instinctive, that he could feel the movement of paper and string at his fingertips without looking. The other man never returned, and no one mentioned what happened to him. So Mustafa found himself with a new job.

Two years after their wedding, Malek was born. Mustafa looked at his son and saw his own childhood recede into the background. As others congratulated him, their pats on the back seemed to push him, faltering into adulthood. It became clear that while Mariam's role was to care for their child, his was to bring home money to meet his family's needs. The store gave him a small raise, and he learned to smile more to increase the tips.

His son's needs grew as quickly as the boy himself did, from diapers to clothes to shoes to school. He would've liked to send Malek to one of the private schools where the children of the Americans, the British, and wealthy Egyptians went. But it was out of the question. What he earned in a year would not even cover half the tuition. Malek went to the same school Mustafa had attended, filled with loud children in overcrowded classrooms and teachers who only wanted to get through each day.

One evening as Mustafa was saying good night to his son, Malek began to tell him about a new building near his school. Malek raised his arms over his head as high as he could stretch them and said, "It's going to be this tall." Then, exhaling, he added with certainty, "Someday, I'm going to build tall buildings like that." Mustafa felt the inside of his body contract, leaving a hollow space. He patted his son gently and said, "May Allah make all your dreams come true."

A few weeks later when Mustafa got to work, his coworkers were huddled in a conversation. No one had put out the pastries or bothered to turn on the lights. They hardly noticed Mustafa when he came in.

As Mustafa started to get the store ready, Ali, one of the

other workers, said to him, "Mustafa, did you hear? Hamid's brother won the lottery."

"What lottery?" asked Mustafa.

"The immigration lottery," Ali answered, waving his hands as if to paint a picture of it. "Hamid's brother is going to America; then he's going to do the paperwork so Hamid can join him."

Mustafa looked at Ali, puzzled, and unable to grasp his words.

Ali took an exasperated breath, and added, "The immigration lottery. Haven't you heard of it, Mustafa? America has a lottery and accepts fifty thousand people into the country every year."

"Fifty thousand from Egypt?" asked Mustafa.

"No, no, fifty thousand from all over the world," said Ali, "but Egypt gets the highest number, and now Hamid will go to America."

Hamid was a young man, in his twenties, who came in every day to sweep and clean the store, the job Mustafa had when he first started. Slowly, Mustafa put the pieces together and understood that to enter this lottery you filled out a simple form, and if your name was picked, you could go to America. It sounded like a fairy tale to him. He knew some of the wealthy managed to immigrate, probably because they had money and connections. But this lottery was open to everyone.

Mustafa glimpsed himself in the glass that reflected the pastries. He was thirty-five years old. His moustache lay thick above his upper lip, but his hairline was beginning to recede, and his black hair was thinning. His cheeks were a bit drawn, and he didn't have to look closely to see that his brown eyes looked faded. Still, perhaps it wasn't too late, he thought. Other people left this life and started over, people like Hamid's brother. Mustafa's body was slender and sinewy, still holding some of the energy of his youth. Perhaps he could take his chances.

In early fall, when the lottery was announced, Mustafa went to the embassy and stood among the hundreds that gathered each day to fill out the required form. There were men wearing *galabiyas* and men wearing expensive suits. He noticed one man in the middle of the line who was well dressed. He kept looking at his watch, which sparkled in the bit of sun crawling through the windows. The man was fidgety, glancing from side to side, shifting his balance as if he were caught in some maze that he knew he couldn't escape. Another man further down the line stood quietly, occasionally tipping his weight from one foot to the other. His stomach protruded, stretching the buttons on his white shirt. His face was withdrawn as if he existed completely inside his heavy body.

There were a few women in the line, all of them attractive and well dressed. One woman with shiny black hair that fell gracefully at her shoulders was trying to soothe her young daughter. When the little girl complained she was tired, the mother picked her up and rubbed her back. Then she put her down and handed her some juice when she said she was thirsty. She seemed completely preoccupied with the child, oblivious to the line she was standing in and its purpose.

Mustafa heard a commotion and looked to the front of the line. There was an old man, leaning on a cane. His face was wrinkled in a pattern of lines that slid down his face. Another man had turned to him and said, "Grandfather, get out of the way and give the young men a chance." The old man waved his cane in the air, making those around him step back. "Never," he said, "you're all worth nothing. *I* will go to America." A security guard came over and told them to stand quietly or they would all have to leave.

When Mustafa's turn came, he was handed a form, told to fill it out and hand it back to the clerk. He wrote down his name, his address, and the schools he had attended. "Is this all?" he asked as he held out the form to the clerk. All he received was a mumbled "yes" as the clerk took it from his hand and the form disappeared from his view. "Next," the clerk demanded, and Mustafa had no choice but to relinquish his position in line to the next person. He walked out of the building slowly, thinking it was too simple an act to change anything.

He told no one that he had applied, not even his wife. He had planned to tell her, but when he got home, Mariam was busy making dinner and Malek was sitting at the table doing homework. The small apartment was quiet. He opened his mouth to say something, and Mariam turned toward him. But he hesitated, unwilling to disrupt their daily routines. He inhaled the air with its unuttered sounds, and Mariam returned her gaze to the food she was cooking. After all, he thought, probably nothing will come of it.

He knew it would be months before he heard anything, and he tried not to think about it. But when the Americans came into the store, he found himself staring at them, wondering what it would be like to live among them. The men were tall, their shoulders held back and their eyes looking straight ahead. They seemed distant from the earth on which they walked. Not like Egyptian men whose shoulders curved in as if weighed down by an invisible load and whose eyes kept drifting to the ground. He watched the Egyptian woman from America when she came in. She always spoke English with her daughters. Would Malek learn English and no longer be able to speak to him? His coworkers had to call his name twice before he responded and focused his attention on wrapping the package in front of him.

Other days, Mustafa felt his heart beat faster with the possibility of actually going to America. Malek would become the engineer he wanted to be and build tall buildings. They would live in a house like the ones on the American shows his wife watched on their black and white television. The excitement rushed through his body like the pulse of an electric shock, until it was a strain to hold still behind the counter.

When a letter arrived from the embassy, he opened it alone, his body shivering although it was a warm day. His eyes skimmed the page not catching a single word, and he had to start again, forcing himself to read each sentence aloud. His name had been picked. He read it over and over, until his head pounded with the words.

At the end of the letter, there was an appointment time and a list of items he was required to bring with him, including his birth certificate, his high-school diploma, and proof of his vaccinations. Mustafa gathered the items over the next few days. Every time he thought to tell Mariam, his tongue became weighed down, the words too heavy to release.

He arrived at the embassy one hot afternoon—the air sticking to his skin—and walked into the stiff air conditioning of the building. He was told to take a seat among the rows of hard plastic chairs. There were people already sitting, a few empty seats between each person. Mustafa slipped his body into one of the chairs, the hard edges scraping against his arms and legs. He sat with his back straight and his hands on his lap. Everyone else was sitting in a similar position. It was quiet in the large room, each person wrapped in their own thoughts, waiting their turn.

When Mustafa's name was called, he was ushered into a small office where a blond man wearing glasses sat behind a desk. The man looked young, perhaps only in his twenties. Mustafa thought there was something familiar about him and wondered if he had come into the pastry store. Distracted by trying to place him, he didn't hear the first words the man spoke to him. "Excuse me," said Mustafa. The man stared at Mustafa then repeated the question, asking him to state his name and place of birth. The man spoke Arabic with a thick accent, and Mustafa had to focus to understand him. The questions only asked him to repeat the information on the various documents he had brought with him. When it was over, the man simply told him he would be receiving another letter with further instructions.

Mustafa left, walking past the chairs, aware of people's eyes following him as if they could decipher some secret by watching him. He felt as if he had been stripped of something, all the papers that marked his identity left behind in that office. The humid air wrapped around his body as he stepped outside and headed back to work.

Several weeks later, Mustafa received another letter with an appointment date. This time he wasn't asked to bring anything. He entered the same room and was again told to take a seat on one of the hard chairs. He noted that there seemed to be fewer people in the room. Each of them sat looking down as if rooted to that spot of earth. The silence became palpable, and Mustafa felt himself drowning in it until he was pulled out each time the guard called out a name, his voice piercing the air like the harsh ringing of a school bell.

When Mustafa's turn came, he was taken into another small office where an older man with gray hair was sitting behind the desk. His small blue eyes squinted at Mustafa when he walked in. The man nodded toward the chair, and Mustafa sat down.

"Why do you want to go to America?" the man asked, looking down at a piece of paper as if he were reading the question.

The question shook Mustafa, making him move closer to the edge of his seat. "I . . . I want to have a better life," he answered.

"What will you do in America?" the man asked without acknowledging the previous answer.

Mustafa shifted his body in the seat and wondered if there was some way he could have prepared for this interview. He felt like he was taking a test for which he hadn't studied. "I will work hard," he responded.

The man looked at him steadily as if waiting for something else then asked, "And what kind of work can you do?"

"I will do any kind of work," he answered.

The man moved one corner of his mouth as if doubting

Mustafa's honesty. "You work in a pastry shop wrapping sweets, is that correct?" he questioned him.

"Yes," said Mustafa, intertwining his fingers to keep them from trembling.

"We don't have that kind of work in America," the man announced.

It wasn't a question, but the man paused as if waiting for an answer.

"I will work at any job. I will work hard," said Mustafa.

"That will be all," the man said as he closed the file in front of him.

Mustafa began to lift his body out of the chair then felt himself being pulled down again. "Will I be allowed to go to America?" he asked.

"You will receive a letter with the final decision," the man stated, his back slightly turned to Mustafa as he placed the file in a drawer.

"But I won the lottery." The words tumbled out of Mustafa's mouth.

The man turned to settle his eyes directly on Mustafa. "America has the right to choose who to let into its country."

Mustafa waited and worked. The store was busy as the school year came to an end. There was a heightened energy in the city as students waited to find out their final test scores, which like a crystal ball would reveal their future. Parents came in to order cakes and pastries. They favored the French pastries for their celebrations. Mustafa wrapped the cakes and the boxes of assorted sweets. It was harder to wrap the French pastries, since you couldn't turn them upside down to twist the string like the Egyptian sweets, which held their shape, and he had to maneuver both paper and string while keeping the box upright.

The days moved rapidly, and the busy time at work made it easier for Mustafa to keep his thoughts still. The last words of the man at the embassy had numbed him. It felt like the day he got his tonsils removed, the ache heavy in his throat, subduing any desire to speak. He assumed now that the final answer would be a rejection; he would not be allowed to go to America. He was glad he hadn't told anyone, not even Mariam, that he had kept it inside himself.

The summer heat stretched into longer days, and most people came into the store late in the evening when the sun had set and a slight breeze enticed them to go out for a walk. They ordered ice cream and filled up the store and the sidewalk in front as they ate and chatted, released from the grip of the day's heavy heat. When he came home one evening, Mustafa found the letter in the mailbox. He was surprised to see it, having almost forgotten that it would arrive. He held it, looking at its official embassy stamps and noted that it was thin, probably not more than one page. He folded it and tucked it into his back pocket.

Two days went by, and Mustafa was tempted to simply throw the letter out, to turn back time as if he had never put his name in the lottery. On the third day while Mariam and Malek were not home, he took out the letter, smoothed its creases, and hesitated. He could let it go, forget the whole thing had happened. But his fingers itched, and he found himself running his fingertips under the seal of the envelope. He pulled out the sheet of paper, braced himself with one solid breath, and told himself that it would be a rejection.

He unfolded the letter and allowed his eyes to run over the words on the page. He had been accepted and his papers would be prepared for him, the papers that would allow him to obtain a visa to the United States. The letter shook in his hands. He folded it quickly, missing the original creases, then shoved it back in the envelope and into his pocket. He had been accepted, and he could bring his family with him. Mustafa took the letter out again, thinking he might have misread the words. He looked at it, reading it aloud to ensure the accuracy of his eyes, and it was true. He could go to America.

Mustafa held the news inside himself, reluctant to tell anyone, afraid he would get another letter saying it was all a mistake. But no more letters came, and his acceptance was like a crumb caught in his throat. He thought about the next steps he would have to take. First he would get his visa, and then he would have to come up with the money for the plane ticket. He had no savings and owned nothing. They lived from month to month on what he earned at the pastry shop. They paid rent for their apartment, and he didn't own a car. There was nothing he could sell. He would have to borrow, perhaps a little from his father and his father-in-law. Maybe he could get another job or work extra hours at the shop. If he went to America alone at first, Mariam and Malek could move in with his parents so they wouldn't have to keep paying rent. Maybe he could ask for a loan from the manager at the shop.

He spent a few days counting and calculating. It might be possible to come up with enough money for his plane ticket. But there would be nothing extra. He would arrive in America with a few pounds in his pocket; once exchanged for dollars, they would become only coins that you might hand a beggar. Mariam and Malek would stay behind until he earned enough money to bring them.

It was a hot August afternoon as Mustafa stood behind the counter in the pastry shop. The shop was air conditioned, but every time someone opened the door, a cloud of heavy humid air entered the store. He looked through the windows. The intense heat made the sidewalks shimmer like a mirage. His vision blurred when he looked outside, forcing him to blink several times in order to refocus on his immediate surroundings. August was the hottest month in Cairo, the air heavy and still like a solid weight everyone carried as they walked. Even the evenings brought no relief, with barely a breeze to release the body from its captivity.

The shop was quiet with only the rare customer coming in.

Everyone seemed tired, and some of the workers were dozing, startled awake only when the door opened. Mustafa looked at the clock. It was one thirty. His appointment to pick up his paperwork from the embassy was in a half hour. Those papers would open the door for him.

Mustafa pictured himself at the airport, moving through the lines, holding his visa, his passport getting stamped. He would be allowed to move from one line to the next until he arrived at the plane. He would go in, take his seat, and wait for the plane to take off. It was quarter to two. If he left now and took a taxi, he could get to the embassy on time. Mustafa looked down at his hands waiting for the next package to wrap and released his breath. The plane would begin moving down the runway, then slip away from the ground and take off. He saw himself suspended in the sky, unable to imagine his landing.

Cumin and Coriander

The oil splattered as she slipped another falafel patty into the frying pan. One drop stung her cheek and she brushed the pricking sensation by rubbing her shoulder against it. Faten was almost finished. The stuffed cabbage was done, the vegetable *tagen* needed just a few more minutes in the oven, and the spinach phyllo triangles were all set on the counter. Once she fried the rest of the falafel, she would be able to pack up and go to the next house.

Mr. David's kitchen was large, with lots of counter space and a new oven that worked easily. The gas was hooked up so she didn't have to worry about replacing the *butagaz* cylinder. The American University in Cairo had built this new building in luxury style. Mr. David's apartment had a huge terrace, almost as large as the apartment itself, with a view of Zamalek's landscape of old villas. Sometimes, Faten would take a minute to step out onto the terrace and let her eyes roam over the city. Despite the growing population and the many new buildings, most of the villas had been able to salvage at least a small garden with orange or guava trees and perhaps some flowers. There were also several new boutiques like Mobaco, Concrete, and New Man, where the upper class and foreigners shopped. Faten preferred being in the kitchen, the feeling of space around her as she maneuvered, a circular dance from refrigerator to counter to oven.

She took out the last falafel, still crackling from the hot oil, and placed it on the paper towel along with the rest. It was almost two o'clock. She was running late and would have to hurry. She wondered if she should spend the two pounds on a taxi to go downtown or if she should wait for the minibus that cost forty piasters. She looked at the money Mr. David had left for her—forty pounds when he owed her only thirty-five: twenty for the food and fifteen for her salary. He was always generous. She would take a taxi. This morning she had been late because she got into an argument with the taxi driver who stopped for her. He had arrogantly insisted that she pay him four pounds when she knew that two was fair. Finally, he waved his hand, encircling the whole area of Imbaba, and stated with assurance that any foreigner he picked up would pay him no less than five pounds. She muttered under her breath, "God save us and protect us," and told the man to go on and find his foreigner; she did not want to delay him.

Faten took the vegetable *tagen* out of the oven and placed it alongside the rest of the food. Then she covered everything with tin foil since she knew Mr. David would not be home for a while. She was grateful to be working for him. He was a young man and not married. He never complained about what she cooked or how she cooked it. Often, he would not give her a list for the next week and accepted whatever choices she made for him. How lucky, she thought, the woman who would marry him. Not like Mr. John, who insisted she use less and less oil. Now he only left her two drops to cook with. And when he was home, he would hover about her. How did he expect her to make the phyllo or the eggplant with no oil? The food came out dry and brittle, nothing to soften the palate, to make one desire it. She wanted to stop cooking for him, but she was reluctant to give up any of her jobs. She didn't know what might happen tomorrow.

She still hoped that she might be able to take her daughter, Houria, out of the public school and put her in the private school with her brother, Mahmoud. *Houria*—it meant freedom. When her son was born, her husband filled out the birth certificate and afterwards told her the child's name. Then, she became "Om Mahmoud," the mother of Mahmoud. She had not expected anything different for the second child. Instead, her husband came in after she had given birth. The room was still spinning, and the walls seemed fluid, waving back and forth with the motion of a belly dancer. He held her hand and smiled. "Well," he said, "do you have a name for our daughter?" She immediately said, "Houria," without thinking it through. Her husband looked a little surprised, but he nodded and said, "It's an old name but good." The name, which meant freedom, had been popular during times of war: 1948, 1967, 1973. What brought it to her mind now, she wondered, when there was peace?

Her husband had insisted on sending Mahmoud to a private school, even though they didn't have much money. After her husband died, she worked hard to continue paying the school fees. Maybe now with the new jobs she had gotten, there might be a chance of transferring Houria. She had been lucky. Maybe her husband was still watching over her. The only job she could find after his death was working as a maid for an Egyptian woman. Then an American professor moved in next door. Faten started cleaning for her. One day, Miss Carol came home with bags of groceries. Faten asked her if she would like her to cook anything. When Miss Carol asked if she knew how to cook, Faten paused at the peculiarity of the question, finally replying, "I can cook anything you want." Miss Carol recommended her for other jobs, cooking for the foreign professors teaching at the American University in Cairo. Soon she had enough to fill her days, often cooking for two people a day. She quit cleaning for the Egyptian woman and became a full-time cook. The pay was better, and she could be in the kitchen by herself. Most of the foreigners never disturbed her. A few of them gave her a small radio to listen to while she cooked, and sometimes she would sing. But summers were hard since most of them traveled, and she could only hope they would give her something extra for that time.

Faten slipped off her long *galabiya,* now spotted with grease and tomato sauce. She reminded herself that next time she would take it home to wash, but she knew she would probably forget. She pulled the long black skirt on over her head, then the sweater over her thin chemise.

She went to the small bathroom and started to tie the black scarf over her head. She caught her face in the square mirror above the sink: her nose took up a little too much space and her face seemed so round. But she was surprised by the blush on her cheeks—it must have come from the hot kitchen. Her lips were full, drawn with precision. Once, one of the women she worked for had told her she was beautiful. Faten stared at her, puzzled. The woman continued, complimenting her smooth brown skin, her clear complexion. "The beauty of your face," she said.

Her husband had thought so too. He would touch his hand to her face and tell her she was as beautiful as the moon. She would smile hesitantly then slip his hand away, feeling embarrassed as if she had been caught in an illicit act. He was gentle, more than she had expected. She did not mind staying at home, taking care of the house, the children. The market nearby was good with clean, fresh produce, not the shriveled tomatoes and rotten fruit in other parts of the city. A breeze traveled through their small balcony, and sometimes, as she swept, a slip of wind would caress her arm. Then, so many times, at the beginning of the month when her husband got paid, he would come home with small gifts for the children and something for her, a scarf bright with a pattern of orange and purple, or a purse, or, once, even perfume. How she raved at his extravagance, buying such gifts when they could barely afford the school fees. He would wave her away and say, "Woman, don't you deserve something in your life?"

Yet, there were days when he returned home quiet, his shoulders stooped, refused anything to eat, and just sat on the balcony smoking a cigarette. "This country," he would say, "does not respect the man who works." She didn't understand and could only tell him that everything would be all right and bring him a cup of tea with mint.

Faten saw again the face in the mirror. She shook her head and reprimanded herself. "Look at you, in your late thirties, a widow with two children and you're thinking of your beauty." Why, she wondered, had her parents named her Faten, after the actress Faten Hamama? Surely they hadn't wished her to become an actress—what a disgrace that would be. It was the word *Hamama* that always intrigued her: a strange name meaning a dove. She imagined a white dove flying into the clouds, losing its outline.

She finished wrapping the scarf over her hair, now streaked with a few lines of gray. She had to hurry and get to Mr. Nicholas's and Madame Kristine's. Since she was running late, she hoped they would have nothing unexpected for her. So strange they had been. That first time she went, Madame Kristine made her sit down and insisted on giving her a cup of tea, then she had gone on and on in her bit of broken Arabic about how they never had a maid or a cook and they wanted her to be happy and to tell them about whatever she needed. She smiled, trying to grasp what she could of the words. Then they started leaving dishes in the sink, which she had to wash before she could cook. And sometimes she was asked to do the laundry. Last week, she spent the whole day there cooking phyllo, grape leaves, tahini, macaroni, and more because they were having a party.

Faten went back to the kitchen, put the money in her purse, then checked the list of food she was making for them. Fava beans—she would have to pick those up on the way there at one of the kiosks then spice them at the house.

She folded the list and placed it in her pocket. Then she walked to the door and picked up the two shopping bags of food she had bought that morning. She stepped out of the apartment, put one of the bags down, and pulled the door shut, turning the knob to make sure it had locked behind her.

When she arrived, Madame Kristine opened the door with a large smile. She ushered Faten into the kitchen and chatted as she watched her set out the food. Then she walked over to the sink and opened the cabinet underneath it. She smiled, pointed at a plastic tub filled with an assortment of dirty plates and glasses, and said, "Thank you, party food was good." Faten stared at the pile. No one had bothered to rinse the dishes, so there were particles of food and smudges from people scooping with their bread. She looked up at Madame Kristine whose smile had become engraved. Faten nodded, and the woman left the kitchen.

Faten closed the cabinet door and began cooking. She could hear music from the living room, something loud with lots of strings. It moved quickly, and she wondered how anyone could make out the words. She cooked silently, trying to get everything on the stove at once. Only the beans were left, but she didn't feel like making them. So often, the cumin and coriander with the garlic would fill her nostrils, and she would have to stir or beat something hard to keep the images from taking shape.

As she mixed the spices in, she again remembered the day her husband died. The children had been particularly energetic, and it took a long time to get them to fall asleep. Finally, she had been able to make herself a cup of tea and sit on the balcony, looking over the rooftops—so many with makeshift apartments where families made a home. The smell of manure and slaughtered goats reached her from the camel market. Some people came with their camels from the Sudan hoping to sell them; others sold goats and sheep that they slaughtered right there.

The place had become a tourist attraction, and officials were talking about charging an entry fee. Such things the foreigners wanted to see. When she told one of the couples she was working for that she lived in Imbaba, they had said, "Oh, the camel market." "No camel," she answered and went into the kitchen.

Her memory continued. She had finished drinking her tea on the balcony. It was getting late. Her husband was still not home, and she decided to go to sleep. When he returned, she was already in the midst of a dream. She never remembered what that dream had been, but it was something urgent and immediate that he woke her from. He shook her awake and said, "Woman, it's not even midnight. What are you doing sleeping? Come on, get up and make me some food." So she had heaved her body out of bed and gone to the kitchen. He insisted she heat up some fava beans and add the cheese and *basterma* meat he had bought. They sat at the table together because he wanted her to stay with him. He started eating and asking about the children. At the third or fourth bite, he brought his right hand to his left arm and started rubbing it. "My arm, Faten, my arm hurts," he said. As she went to him, his head fell onto his shoulder, and that was all.

Faten shook herself a little to come out of the memory. She was looking for a bowl to put the beans in but couldn't find one. Then she remembered the dishes. She opened the cabinet and saw several dirty bowls. She stared, and her shoulders rose with one heavy breath. Then she lifted the tub of dishes, placed it by the sink, and began to scrub.

The Silver Platter

That morning, the sun stretched an orange streak across the sky. Nageh had felt its bright salute against his eyes, causing him to wake a little earlier than usual. He had left the shutters open the previous night, liking the way the full moon penetrated through the window, casting a shadow of light across his room. After he had slipped under the covers, his mother had come in and closed the shutters, assuming he had forgotten. Shortly after she left, he got up to re-open them.

He prepared for work, adjusting his tie and suit jacket in front of the small mirror above his dresser, the same mirror where he had looked years earlier to find the hairs just beginning to create stubble across his chin. Now his clean-shaven face stared back. He hesitated for a moment, noting how his brown eyes with their hint of hazel seemed to brighten his complexion this morning. The mirror only showed down to his shoulders, but he frowned at the narrowness of his physique, his body still seeming boyish in its appearance. He finished getting ready and went to the kitchen where he ate a small bowl of beans and some bread that his mother had prepared the previous evening, knowing he liked to get an early start.

The day was just beginning to unfold as he began his walk to the bus stop. Nageh's family had moved to the suburb of Maadi just five years ago in 1963, but already the area was rapidly becoming more crowded. Nageh enjoyed the quiet of the early morning before the carts and taxis began to fill the streets. Although it was the Coptic month of Amsheer, the sand had not yet drifted in with the wind, and the air still felt clean, especially at this hour of the day. He rounded the corner past the barbershop where he got his hair cut, past the butcher where his mother purchased meat, and past the coffee shop where his father spent his evenings. A little farther on, he went by the street where his two elder brothers lived, both now married and settled into their lives. It seemed strange to think that just two years ago, they had all been living in the house together, arguing over who was the best looking and sometimes whispering at night about the girls they liked. He felt abandoned as each of them married and went on to start his own home. The silence they left behind filled the rooms, as most evenings it was just he and his mother since his father preferred to frequent the coffee shop to smoke his *shisha* and play backgammon.

As he neared the bus stop, he wondered about his own future. He was approaching thirty, still a young man, but he knew that soon his family would expect him to begin thinking about marriage and settling down. He had watched as each of his brothers left behind the young women they had pursued when they went out in the evenings and chose instead from among those considered to be acceptable wives presented to them by the family.

Checking his watch, he saw that he would arrive at the bank about fifteen minutes early. He wondered if Noor would be there. She was usually the first teller to arrive, and when he came in, she greeted him with a courteous, "Good Morning, Mr. Yusef." He usually responded politely, but a few weeks ago, he had stopped to ask, "How are you today, Noor?" They had begun to talk, brief conversations that allowed them to crack open the door into each other's lives. Noor's family lived in Old Cairo, a poorer section of the city unlike the more middle-class neighborhoods of Maadi. Her family was part of the working class, just making their living. Noor explained that she had felt lucky when her exam scores were good enough to admit her to the Business School at the University of Cairo. She had graduated just last year, and this position as teller in the bank was a step that would help to improve her family's life.

Nageh liked to listen to the lilt of her voice, the way her words created a rhythm of notes rising and falling. She was dark-complexioned, clearly with a background from Upper Egypt. But he found the deeper shade of her skin attractive, and she moved her body with a certain confidence, oblivious to the eyes that had determined that beauty was enhanced by lighter skin. Her short dark hair framed her face, and he liked to see her broad smile, the way it made her eyes shine. She was quite slender, not like most women whose bodies curved sensually as they walked, aware of the eyes that followed them. Yet she seemed more substantial than other women, as if she held some inner peace that he still found elusive.

Their conversations had lengthened over the past few weeks. And with an invisible understanding, they both appeared at work a little earlier each morning, no one noting the change except perhaps the security guard who opened the bank doors for them.

Nageh entered the bank to find Noor taking her coat off, having arrived only moments before him.

"Good morning," he said.

She turned, seeming a little startled by his voice. "Good morning," she answered.

"Did you have a good holiday yesterday?" he asked, referring to Friday, their one day off each week when the bank closed.

"Yes, it was a quiet day," she said. "How about you?"

"Not so quiet," he said. "My brothers both came over."

There was always a slight formality to their conversations in the bank even when no one else was there, as if the desks had ears to eavesdrop on them. Yet each day, Nageh felt like he was taking one step closer, slipping toward something delightful yet with a feeling of trepidation that he could easily find himself hanging on the edge of a cliff. This morning he took a small bar of Cadbury chocolate out of his briefcase and presented it to Noor, who clearly blushed at receiving the gift. There were only a few select stores that sold the imported chocolates, and Nageh had gone out of his way to find one.

"I thought you might need something sweet today," he said, surprised at his own forwardness.

"Thank you," she said. "It's very kind of you."

The other employees began entering the bank, and Nageh quickly made his way to his office. He was one of the assistant managers who spent the day adjusting numbers, discussing the bank's investments and meeting with important customers. It was a good job, and he was treated respectfully by the other managers, despite being a Copt. They wished him a good holiday on Christmas and Easter, allowing him to take a few extra days off, and he offered them good wishes at Ramadan. He knew he was fortunate as there were other banks where Copts were never allowed to move into managerial positions.

That afternoon as he settled to drink the tea his mother had made after lunch, his father sat across from him and cleared his throat. Nageh straightened his back against the chair and took a quick sip of his tea, the hot liquid slightly burning his tongue.

"How is the job, Nageh?" his father asked as he leaned forward and placed his glass of tea on the table.

"It's good, thank God. They're happy with my work," Nageh answered, crossing his legs and trying to anticipate what his father's conversation might lead to.

"That's good news, Nageh. I'm pleased that you found good work and you're beginning to get settled in your life," his father said, reaching for the tea but only to wrap his hands around the warm glass.

"Yes," responded Nageh quietly. He waited for his father to speak again.

His father shifted slightly in his chair, then drank the rest of his tea in three sips, placed the glass firmly back on the table, and began to speak. "You're approaching thirty years, and you have a good job in your hand, and you're saving your money. Now you have to begin to build your life. Have you thought about marriage?"

Although he had been expecting it, the question still caught Nageh off guard, and he felt the hard slats of the chair pressing into his back. "Yes, father," he answered, knowing it was not an adequate response.

His father continued as if he had been given a signal to proceed. "Nagy, there are many young women who are the right age from good families and ready to marry."

Nageh disliked the shortened version of his name and the way it seemed to revert him back to childhood. He leaned forward in the chair. "Yes, father," he repeated, "but if possible, just give me a little time to think."

"Ok, my son," his father said, "but don't take too long or you'll find yourself getting old."

Sunday was usually a quiet day at the bank. Nageh had felt relieved when he entered and saw Noor; something in him had feared he would not find her that morning. She smiled in greeting, and they proceeded with their morning conversation.

The day drifted slowly, and with few customers coming in, the employees began their usual gossiping. When Noor left for her morning break, Nageh caught the whispers of the other tellers: ". . . acts like a queen" . . . "her nose up in the air" . . . "thinks herself beautiful and her color dark like mud" . . . "look at her so skinny, all bones" . . . "her family from upper Egypt can't find enough to eat" . . ."she sways when she walks but there is nothing to shake" . . ."of course looking for a husband" . . ."her name means light but who's going to marry those dark bones."

Nageh closed his door to block out their banter. He had heard them before and knew that their silly gossip was just a way to pass the day, but it bothered him that they chose Noor as the focus of their harsh words. Each day, he watched her exchange only a few quiet sentences with the other tellers; she seemed aware that they had pushed her to the fringes of their circle. When she returned, they greeted her with their plastered smiles and resumed the habits of their work.

Nageh left a little later than usual and chose to take the long walk home, foregoing the crammed bus ride. His father's words of marriage intermingled with the tellers' voices. What did he want in a wife? Someone like his mother, setting the table each day with food and managing the household while he went to work? His life would continue as it was, except the woman greeting him at the end of the day would be his wife instead of his mother. There must be another option. The possibility of a companion, someone he could share his thoughts with, maybe travel, something beyond the domesticity he saw in the lives around him. He loved to hear Noor's observations, the way she noticed the details around her as if they were brand new and the way she seemed immune to the materialistic pursuits of the other women. He knew she was dark and thin, but when he looked at her, he saw a beauty that pleased him.

He looked up for a minute to veer away from the shoppers who were beginning to fill the late afternoon streets. There was another obstacle that he kept tucked in his mind, not wanting to consider it, the reason he had not stepped beyond the bounds of their morning conversations. That Noor was Muslim and he was Christian was something he preferred to ignore, convincing himself that there was nothing between them beyond friendly talk. But now his father's urging toward marriage forced him to untuck that piece of information and look at it more closely. Could he even marry a Muslim woman? Converting was impossible for her. If she agreed to marry him, he would have to convert. His marriage would never be recognized by the church. Did she love him enough? What if they left the country? And how would their families react? Did it really matter if they wanted to spend their lives together? The questions agitated him, and he looked around to distract himself. Turning a corner, he noticed the bakery and stopped to buy some bread, the round loaves having just been delivered fresh and steaming, before walking the last street toward home.

Nageh didn't arrive early at the bank for the next three days. He came in on time after most of the employees had already occupied their spaces. Noor's glance toward him as he walked through the door was almost imperceptible. Yet, he felt her question pour into his skin each morning. He let the day's work take him over. The numbers, the books to balance, assets, loans, interest—these were the things he had trained himself to control. By the third day, he felt himself sinking, as if the air in his office had gathered weight and tightened its grip around his body till he felt he could never rise again.

He sat still that afternoon, almost unable to get up as the other employees went home, responding to their queries with "just one more thing to finish before leaving." Until, without looking up, he knew that only he and Noor were left in the building.

He raised his eyes, and this time there was nothing subtle about the glance she directed toward him. He piled his papers neatly on the desk and gathered his belongings.

Stepping into the lobby, his remark was a clear invitation, "Good afternoon, Noor."

"Good afternoon, Mr. Yusef," she responded, although it sounded more like a question.

Nageh inhaled, felt his breath go inside his body, and finally released it with the question that had been nudging him for the past three days. "Would you like to take a walk, perhaps get something to eat? And please call me Nageh."

He received her smile in response.

It was still early in the evening, so the small café on the Nile *corniche* was not crowded. They sat at a small table at the edge of the terrace, looking over the water, its surface just beginning to flicker as the light shifted in the sky. They spoke hesitantly about work at the bank, Nasser's decreasing popularity after the war, the sweet taste of the lemonade they were drinking, until Nageh ventured with a small comment, saying, "I enjoy spending time with you." Then they were able to wind their way into a more private channel, not so much words as tone and gesture. Nageh offered a vision of spending their lives together as if he were suggesting a day's outing and Noor agreed to the plan. As the evening sun settled, marking the silhouettes of the felucca sails against the water, their understanding was clear.

After saying goodbye, Nageh crossed over the Qasr el Nil Bridge to catch his bus. People mingled on the bridge, delaying their journeys. He noted the couples huddled together, leaning against the railing overlooking the Nile, but their faces were turned toward each other, the water lapping invisibly in the darkness below them. Nageh imagined himself and Noor like these couples, but something tugged at his imagination, keeping him from calling up the vision fully. They had spoken of their desire to be together but without delving into the details, which now emerged in Nageh's mind. There will be a way to make it work, he said to himself firmly and kept walking across the bridge to the other side, refusing to be distracted by the activity surrounding him.

On Friday, Nageh stayed in bed later than usual. He lingered in his room while his parents went into their normal routine, his mother already beginning to prepare for the midday meal when his brothers and their wives would come over and join them. Nageh knew he couldn't put off the conversation with his father. The necessity of it nagged at his brain so he couldn't concentrate on anything else. He found his father on the balcony eating white pumpkin seeds, cracking the shells between his teeth in a steady rhythm.

"*Sabah el kheir,*" Nageh said as he stepped onto the balcony and slipped into a chair.

"*Sabah el noor,* Nagy. How are you?" responded his father, adjusting his posture slightly.

"Thanks be to God," Nageh said, trying to control his heart's palpitations.

A pause followed, his father gesturing toward the bowl of seeds, but Nageh shook his head. Below them, they could hear the playful voices of the young boys beginning to gather in the street. Inevitably, a soccer game would ensue with much noise and shouting.

"Father," Nageh began.

His father raised his eyes and paused in his eating. Nageh knew he would have to continue.

"There is a young woman at the bank, and I . . . she . . . I have feelings for her."

Now his father looked solidly at him, his eyes direct and almost piercing, making Nageh wish he could recapture his words.

"Who is she?" asked his father.

Nageh rubbed his neck as he sought for what he wanted to say. "Her name is Noor. She is one of the tellers."

His father proceeded to his next question, "Who is her family?"

The question had come too soon, although Nageh knew he should have anticipated it. Now it suspended itself in the air between them.

"They live in Old Cairo, but they are a good working family," Nageh responded, trying to keep his tone steady.

"What is the family's name?" persisted his father.

Nageh's eyes strayed down, noting the fraying cuffs of his pants, realizing he would soon need to go to the tailor for a new pair.

"It's Abd el Karim," he said.

"Abd el Karim," his father repeated as if testing the words on his tongue, "That is a Muslim name," he said, his tone partially a question.

"Yes," Nageh answered, the word falling from his mouth, silencing even the escalating noise on the street below.

"You want to marry a Muslim girl?" His father's back straightened away from the chair, and he leaned forward. "You have your cousins on both sides, beautiful young women to choose from, and the daughters of families we have befriended for years that are all available to you, and you leave all that to go and choose a Muslim woman. To insult and betray our home. This will not happen."

His father's eyes sparked as he spoke, and Nageh felt the heat enter his body till it seemed he could no longer contain it. But his father leaned back with his last words indicating the conversation had closed.

When his brothers arrived with their wives, Nageh remained on the edges. He sat in the room with the men but added little to the discussion. He felt his body to be an empty shell, hollowed out.

At the table everyone sat together, serving the chicken and stuffed zucchini and eggplant his mother had spent the day cooking.

"God bless your hands, Mother. The food is excellent," said his older brother.

"Yes," his wife added. "Honestly, this is the best eggplant I've had."

The compliments proceeded around the table as Nageh's mother responded and pressed each person to eat, adding more to their plates.

As the meal came to a close, Nageh saw his father lean toward his eldest brother with a whisper.

His brother's response was louder. "Yes, I know her. Her family is from Asyut. Working class. They have just enough, only what they need. She is skinny and dark."

"Who? Who is she?" asked his mother.

His father looked up and appeared to be taking a moment to arrange his thoughts before speaking. Then he laid his words evenly on the table. "It seems our son has been trying to find his own bride and this is what he has found—a girl who is Muslim and from a family that is poor. And now my oldest son tells me she's dark and skinny. This is our son's choice for a wife."

"What! What are you saying?" his mother voice rose. "Our son has a hundred beautiful women to choose from. Good girls from good families and we know them. Why would he choose someone like this?"

Nageh felt the strength of their eyes all on him. But it seemed he had lost any words that he might speak.

His oldest brother addressed him directly. "What's going on Nageh? It's impossible that this girl is attractive to you. You must be feeling sorry for her. You always were the sensitive one among us. It's not just that she's Muslim—this is impossible in our family—but she is dark and skinny. There is nothing of beauty in her. What could you see in her?"

Nageh cleared his throat and tried to respond. "She is a good girl, and I like her. I . . . I love her, and I want to marry her."

"Oh my God, Oh my God, Oh my God," his mother's voice pierced the afternoon. "My son is going to marry a Muslim woman—And what will we do? I won't have a son. And she is also skinny and dark—What will your children look like? Why would you do this to them? Is this a choice? My son, think of your future. It is impossible—impossible—impossible." His mother tore at the neck of her dress and slapped her cheeks. Finally, as her screams and tears exhausted her, Nageh's sisters-in-law came to her side, urging her to calm down.

Nageh's middle brother, who had remained quiet, now turned toward him. "Nageh, think carefully. Is this something you want to do? There is no return in a decision like this. And there is no way for you to marry her without converting to become a Muslim like her. You would no longer be a part of our family. It is impossible. Is this what you want?"

His mother's laments became a refrain behind his brother's words, and Nageh felt the swirling of their voices in his head. Almost inaudibly, he said, "I'm going to rest now," and got up to return to his room.

Nageh arrived at the bank on time the next day and remained in his office on the pretext of too much work. Although he felt Noor's presence and her occasional gaze, he kept his eyes focused only at the work on his desk.

His thoughts gathered slowly over the next few days. On Thursday, he came in early and Noor was there; clearly she had been arriving at their usual time every morning.

"Noor . . . ," he started to speak even before he reached her, extracting each word slowly. "The situation will not work—the differences between us—my family can't approve . . ."

His words faltered and there was nothing else he could offer. He tried to look more fully into Noor's face, but when he saw the sadness that veiled her features, he couldn't sustain his gaze.

Quietly, she said, "Thank you, Mr. Yusef. Have a nice day."

Nageh tried to speak again, but another employee arrived and their privacy evaporated.

A week later, Noor didn't come to work. Throughout the day, he caught the whispering that revealed she had unexpectedly resigned, some saying she had found another job, some saying she was getting married.

When his father approached the topic again, Nageh interrupted him, simply saying, "*Khalas*"—it's finished.

"Good," his father said and nodded.

Nageh ignored his mother's attempts at conversations about women they knew, retreating to his room with an excuse of being tired or having some work to catch up on.

Weeks passed steadily and Nageh kept his thoughts to himself. Being at the bank was a constant reminder as he watched the new girl take over Noor's position. And each night, he returned to his mother's suggestions to introduce him to another girl.

The plan formed slowly inside him. It was 1968 and the country was healing poorly from the war the previous year. Its seams were coming undone, but as a result there were new openings that had not been there before. Nageh caught one of them. Alone, he created a choice for himself, opened a small door of his own free will without anyone's knowledge until everything was complete.

When he told his family that he was immigrating to America, that he had been approved, that he had already bought his ticket, their mouths opened to speak, but he had caught them by surprise. They didn't know whether to be happy or sad, and their words only stumbled. No one in their family had done this, but the rumblings were clear and emigration was already fraying the country's edges, the unraveling it would ultimately cause beginning to manifest itself.

His family's responses fell in a cluttered pile " . . . are you sure . . . but why? . . . you have a good job . . . there are opportunities there . . . they say it's beautiful . . . lots of money."

Nageh didn't answer. He let them talk without him, only announcing the day he was leaving and repeating that he had already submitted his resignation at work. The family's conversation fizzled, the finality of his decision silencing them.

On his last day at work, his coworkers arranged a party in his honor. For a moment, their kind words made Nageh hesitate about his decision, knowing their appreciation for him was sincere. But he reminded himself that everything was in order, that he could not step back now. They presented him with a round silver platter, its rim etched into a design. On the back were engraved the words: *As A Souvenir To Our Dear N. Yusef. With Our Best Wishes. From Your Colleagues Banque De Cairo May 1968.*

He heard their words as he thanked them for the gift: "Good luck Nageh—we envy you—it's a great country. Your name means success—that's why you're going to America."

That evening, Nageh sat in his room looking at the two suitcases he had bought. He could not pinpoint the exact moment of his decision. It seemed as if something had been propelling him in this direction. He knew he could not stay here, continue this life as it had now become. He imagined himself in America—who would he be: a successful banker, no one, just a man working a menial job? Then a flash of a vision: an old man, thin hair, sagging body, hands faded with wrinkles, sitting alone at a table. The image shattered like a premonition in his eyes.

Nageh looked around him. There was the platter on his bed. The surface was shiny and the silver heavy, the best kind. He turned it over and let the words skim across his eyes. Although it was not something he expected to need in America, Nageh wrapped it carefully and placed it in the suitcase.

An Encounter

I lived on the third floor of an apartment building across the street from a school I couldn't see. From my balcony, only the roof of the Mere de Dieu school for girls was visible. It was a gothic brick structure neatly fenced in and further obfuscated by a trail of trees that surrounded the grounds. Afternoons, I would hear the bell in three flat tones. One minute later, there was the stampede of children's feet into the schoolyard, carrying with it their voices like an orchestra in full swing. I could never detect an individual voice or particular words. Rather, they were a group of instruments, at times creating a harmony of even tones, other times disjointed and shrill, but always in unison. During their recess, I would take a break from my work, sit on the balcony sipping a cup of mint tea, for which I had finally acquired a taste, and listen. Usually my meditation was broken by sharp screams like the scratching of a violin string. The sounds would subside for a moment, only to rise again until the bell summoned the children back inside.

My excursion to Egypt had lasted longer than planned. I had arrived four years earlier with a two-year contract to teach at the American University, leaving behind a girlfriend and several part-time positions. It was a welcome relief from shuttling back and forth among different universities, teaching everything from composition to public speaking courses, and once becoming desperate enough to take on a creative writing class at the local prison. The job at the university was a stroke of luck; with only a master's degree and a few years of teaching experience, I was surprised they hired me.

It wasn't difficult to get adjusted: teaching every morning, then hanging about the faculty lounge to chat with the other instructors and make plans for our Friday and Saturday weekend. The university provided me with a furnished apartment in Garden City, only a few minutes walk from campus. The pollution that layered the streets and the difficulty of being understood with my few words of Arabic were a small price, given the comforts of a steady paycheck that enabled me to afford a cook and a housekeeper.

The American University was an oasis in the heart of Cairo, not only with its greenery and flowering plants so unlike the grayness of the city where the sidewalks were dotted with occasional leafless trees, but also with its students who seemed immune to the restrictions of their culture. The women arrived with miniskirts, sleeveless shirts, and hair loose about their shoulders. In the summer, the young men expressed their daring by wearing shorts. Such clothing was an absolute taboo on the city streets where men wore long pants even at the height of the heat, and the majority of women wore scarves snug about their faces and long sleeves regardless of the seasons' changes.

The women at the university were a sight to behold; they looked more prepared for walking down a fashion runway than a university campus. Even their jeans were creased and tailored, and I wondered how long it took to put on their makeup and place each strand of hair in just the right place. I enjoyed greeting them each morning and happily responded to their flirtations. With their smiles and lingering walks across campus, they seemed trained in seduction. It was difficult to remember that they were only about eighteen years old. I wondered how a culture that placed so much emphasis on virginity could train its daughters to dress and act so provocatively. There were times when I was tempted to stretch the flirtation, to see how far the young woman would carry it. But something held me in check. After a while, I realized that for these women, seductiveness was a pose, and I feared the consequences of my intended desires.

After two years, my department acquired a new director who decided we should step ahead into the modern world by using computers in our classes. Since I had no expertise in that area, my request to have my contract renewed was denied. I was reluctant to return to my previous life in the States. And there was the matter of my girlfriend, Kay, who was anticipating that my return would be followed by our wedding. Despite her diligent correspondence and my erratic postcards throughout the previous two years, I could now only conjure her up as the outline of a shadow. Her thin, straight body grew narrower as I considered the voluptuous curves of the women around me. There had been a brief and inconsequential affair with one of my colleagues shortly after I arrived. Our attraction to each other was probably due to both of us having left behind unresolved relationships. There were a few evenings spent horseback riding under the desert moon, a romantic dinner at the Omam Indian restaurant and even a weekend getaway to one of the Red Sea resorts. After that, the department gossip escalated, and it seemed wise to call it off. It was really a mutual decision, although it took some convincing to show Kelly that we were not destined for lifelong partnership.

When my contract wasn't renewed, I had to find work and a new apartment in order to maintain my residency status and remain in Egypt. As the semester neared its end, it seemed there was no alternative but to return home. Yet every time one of my Egyptian colleagues asked, "So, Peeta, what will you do?" I dreaded the departure even more. My name had acquired a twist of language. The English *r* was a little awkward for Egyptians to pronounce, so "Peter" had become "Peeta." It sounded a bit British to my ear, but I rather liked it. As an ordinary Peter, staying within the norm had always sufficed. But with that lingering "a" at the end, new horizons opened. Combined with my students calling me "Doctor," despite my protests, I found my heels lifting off the ground with a bit more buoyancy.

At the last moment when departure seemed imminent, I learned of an editing job at an English-language magazine. *Our Egypt* needed someone to copyedit articles that were either written by nonnative speakers or translated from Arabic. The job paid quite well and seemed simple enough, so I was hired and the necessary paperwork done to keep me in the country. Since the university didn't need the apartment immediately, I was allowed to stay on for a reasonable rent. Soon I realized that copyediting in this case meant rewriting articles that were often truly incomprehensible. *Our Egypt* was a glossy magazine, and no one seemed to mind too much what the articles said as long as the advertisers were happy. So every few days, a young man rang my door to deliver more inarticulate articles and to pick up my revisions of the previous ones.

When the bell gave its last ring at two o'clock, my classmates and I ran out of the building, leaving behind the nuns' voices futilely demanding that we slow down. It was a relief to be away from their watchful French eyes. They seemed to hold us to an invisible standard, but we sensed our inadequacy, knowing that our appearance and behavior, as well as our French pronunciation, inevitably fell short of their expectations.

I always took the long way home, walking further down Kasr el Aini street to the bridge and across to Giza. The main street was more interesting than the quiet back streets that circled through Garden City. At the bus stops, the men paced back and forth on the sidewalk, while the women crowded themselves onto the single bench. Whenever I waited for a minibus, I would reject the women's offer to make room for me. Instead, I remained standing, occasionally stepping forward to see if I could catch sight of the bus.

As I walked, I would hear the men going past me mumble under their breath *"eshta"* or *"sharbat,"* and although I kept walking, it was difficult not to smile just a tiny bit. Their comments felt like compliments, and their words were so sweet. *Eshta* was the cream that rose to the top when we boiled our milk. Some mornings, I would add a little sugar to it, mixing it gently, and eat it on bread with thick strawberry jam. And *sharbat* was the punch served at weddings, a mixture of sweet juices that made it taste like syrup inside your mouth. The more daring men would say something then stare at me trying to break my composure. But in Egypt, men begin making comments to you when you're very young, maybe just twelve or thirteen. So you learn how not to miss a beat in your step, how to keep your eyes set straight; otherwise, if they sense a response, you could be in trouble.

Papa was a doctor so he didn't spend much time at home. But his presence was always there because he set the rules. He had decided I would go to the Mere de Dieu because, he said, a French education would turn me into an elegant young woman. Papa was taller than most men, and sometimes I think it was his height that made other people respect him. He was very strict. Sometimes, he would summon me, saying, "Nermine, come here." His eyes would travel from my hair to my shoes. The next day, if Mama said we were going shopping to buy me new clothes, I knew he had disapproved of something, but I never knew what. Mama didn't work. She had gone to college for two years, then she married so there was no need to continue. She spent a lot of time complaining about our housekeepers and cooks, and it seemed that every few weeks there was someone new dusting our furniture. They forgot to sweep the balcony, she would complain, and now she couldn't sit there to drink her afternoon tea. My mother was thin, her collarbone protruding slightly, and when she was upset, it twitched almost imperceptibly. Mostly, she visited with her sisters and cousins. When she mentioned friends, she had to go back all the way to her school days to remember.

Just one year after my parents married, my older brother, Sadiq, was born. Now he was in America going to college. The plan was that he would return after getting his BA then go to medical school here. It would take him longer, but this way he would have the prestige of an American diploma; at least that's what Papa said. Sadiq sent me a few letters when he first arrived telling me how bad America was, how everyone only thought of themselves and no one helped each other. When I asked him about the women, he said they didn't wear enough clothes and their behavior was sinful. I wanted to know more, but for a long time he didn't write. Then a few weeks ago, I got a short note from him telling me that he had just returned from a vacation with some American friends and that he was thinking of staying through the summer to take extra classes.

The first time I saw him was when I looked up to follow the whistle of a bird. He was standing on a balcony and seemed to be staring right at me. The sun was shining brightly that day, making his brown hair glimmer as if tiny flecks of light were attached to the ends. He didn't seem to be very tall, and he had a slender physique that made him look young. His look caught me off guard, and it was a few moments before I remembered to turn my face away. I felt awkward as I began walking, wondering if his eyes were following me.

No one was home when I returned, and I was glad since I felt a bit out of sorts. As I changed out of my uniform, I wondered how I would compare to those American women. The American TV serials we watched showed everyone hopping in and out of beds, but of course that was immoral. I slipped on one of my favorite dresses, a blue and white one that tied in the back. It fitted around my waist and made me look older than my sixteen years. My parents were not too strict about my clothing as long as I tied my long hair back and kept my dresses below the knee.

The next morning, as I entered school, I turned for a quick look toward the balcony, but I couldn't see anyone. The lessons droned in my ears all day while I kept thinking back to the look on his face as he watched me. It seemed almost as if he was studying me, preparing for an exam. Who was he? I wondered. Probably an American, just staying for a short while. There were stories of women who fell madly in love with American men visiting the country and were swept away in a whirlwind marriage and a flight across the ocean.

That evening as we were eating dinner, I asked my father if I could go to America to study like my brother. He raised his eyes from his plate, put his fork and knife down, then looked at me for almost a minute before he answered. No respectable girl, he said, would allow herself to travel alone to a country like America and certainly no daughter of his. Then he turned his head back to his plate, picked up his fork, and kept eating.

I continued to glimpse him on his balcony, and most times I thought he was looking back, but I would lower my eyes quickly. One day, as I turned the corner beyond school, I heard steady footsteps behind me. When I approached one of the quieter streets, they caught up and it was him standing next to me.

"Hello," Peter said, looking carefully at the young girl and enjoying the way he could detect the curves of her body despite the uniform's attempt to hide them.

"Hello," Nermine replied with a slight pause in the middle of the word that emerged almost like a stutter.

"You go to the *Mere de Dieu?*" he asked, although it was obvious his purpose was not to elicit an answer.

She nodded, her eyes remaining downcast and her feet fixed to their spot.

"What's your name?" he asked.

"Nermine," she replied, her voice just above a whisper.

"Would you like to get an ice cream, a gelato?" he inquired, gesturing in the direction of the pastry shop.

"No, I . . . I need to get home," she said, now willing her feet to move.

But before she could take a step, he extended his hand and said, "My name is Peter. I live right across the street from your school."

"Are you American?" she stammered before she realized what she had asked.

"Yes," he said, opening his face into a broad smile. "Have you been there?"

"No, but my brother goes to college there."

Their steps picked up in unison as they circled the streets of Garden City, once unaware that they had returned to the same spot. He let her go when she announced that she had to catch her minibus.

After that day, each morning, before entering through the school's iron gates, she would look up to find him standing on the balcony, his eyes roving the street. She would flicker a smile, and he would wave back, a slight gesture that could have been mistaken for brushing away a fly.

She sat through the droning voices of her teachers, her mind wondering how she had dared to speak to him, at his easy smile, and the way he succeeded in getting her to talk. Yesterday, she had told him about her family and her life, and he had listened with such interest as if she was different from everyone else. She was relieved when the day came to an end, and she could escape from the walls of the school building.

In the morning, Peter stayed on the balcony until the school bell rang and all the girls were encased inside the gothic structure. She was beautiful, her eyes a shade of honey, with such long lashes he thought they could be her wings. He had enjoyed entering her world for a while as they walked that first day. It was amazing that from the dust of this city, there grew such beautiful women. His work had kept him cooped up in his apartment, and he had little social interaction with anyone, only occasionally visiting the university but finding it awkward to return there after his dismissal.

They fell into a routine. When the dismissal bell rang, she would look up to find him leaning over the balcony, his eyes scanning the street. Once he saw her, he would disappear, and a few minutes later, she would hear his footsteps behind her. They avoided Kasr el Aini Street, instead walking through Garden City. Designed by an engineer who had a fondness for compasses, the streets were a maze of intertwining circles that created the residential neighborhood. They tempted you with the illusion of moving forward, only to find you had been taken back to the beginning of your journey. But she had attended the Mere de Dieu since she was a child and knew most of the streets' secrets, only occasionally missing a turn and having to begin the maze again.

Each afternoon, they talked. He described America to her, and with each story, her curiosity grew. It took on the proportions of a wonderland with its skyscrapers and its abundance of fanciful products. She told him about her simple daily life, but his eager questions transformed it to something tantalizing and magical, till she had to laugh and say, "That's not my life. You're making it a fairytale." And it was her laugh that caught him, tugged at his chest till he felt the muscles stretch. Her eyes brightened and her face shone until he began to believe she was a magic creature.

Back at his apartment, Peter concluded that it was only an

innocent flirtation. He had not even reached to hold her hand. And although she was in school, she was only about ten years younger. It was not such a big thing really. Yet he found himself marking his days with their meetings, planning his routine around them, and looking forward more and more to the sound of her voice. Her life seemed removed from his mundane world, and through her stories, he felt for the first time that he was entering life in this city.

Nermine grew quieter at home, going through the motions of helping her mother with the household tasks and doing her homework. Her parents didn't seem to notice, and she was able to stay in the world of her thoughts, recalling his quickening steps each afternoon as he caught up with her. She liked explaining things to him. He seemed to know so little about Cairo, and she enjoyed playing teacher to his questions. Once, his arm slightly brushed hers, and she felt her body shiver at the unexpected touch. She was afraid someone would see them on the streets, but none of her family lived in Garden City, and there was nothing to bring them there. After her schoolmates dispersed, it seemed safe to walk through the tangled streets, yet her eyes were always watchful.

The first time she went up to his apartment, it seemed inevitable, as if this had been their destination all along. She felt almost giddy at finding herself in an American man's apartment, startled by her own bravery. Peter looked at her and wondered how he had succeeded in bringing her here, to have her among his books and papers as if she was his. Their intimacy was gentle and cautious, each day edging only slightly closer. But his touch pulled her in till she succumbed, and they were wrapped inside each other.

Weeks later, when the door crashed in, they were sitting on the couch and she was in his arms. It was her father and another man who came in, fury painted on their faces as they entered. Their motions were swift and almost predetermined.

Her father snatched her from the couch, spouting words she could barely distinguish—of shame on the family and selling herself cheaply—while the other man confronted Peter with a tone that sounded like a threat. She was pulled out by her father and driven home in silence.

The next day, an early knock woke Peter, and the doorman handed him a registered letter. It was from the Egyptian Embassy informing him that he was no longer a welcome guest in Egypt and was required to leave within two days. If he didn't depart, he would be arrested.

At home, Nermine was pushed into her room and the door locked. Her parents' voices seeped through, and she listened till she could make out the content of their words: ". . . a scandal if anyone finds out . . . should have watched her more carefully . . . lying . . . shameful . . . raised to do this . . . your fault . . . can't let anyone know . . . keep her in school . . . someone escort her both ways . . . no college . . . find a husband soon . . . my reputation." Her father's voice towered over her mother's whimpers, and she could imagine her mother's bones protruding more sharply in response.

Peter paced nervously in the airport's waiting area, the hard plastic chairs keeping him standing. For the last two days, a thin man smoking a cigarette had been watching his apartment and following him the few times he went out. There was little he could do. The airport was dusty, and the waiting area filled mostly with foreigners returning home. He already felt nostalgic for the city he was leaving, but he had called Kay and knew she would be waiting for him when he arrived.

After Nermine had been in her room a week with only the housekeeper bringing in meals, her mother came in and made the announcement that she would be returning to school the next day.

"The doorman will take you there and come to get you at the end of the day. You will tell everyone that you have been sick and you are being escorted because of your health." Before retreating, her mother turned to add, "It's a shame really. You were such a beautiful girl and now you're ruined."

The next day as Nermine approached the school building, she didn't need to look up to know that the balcony was empty.

Backgammon

My mother tugged at my small hand. She was done negotiating her purchase of the material she was buying to make new living-room curtains. The store was crowded, and we had waited outside for the order. While she looked at the decorated shop window, I watched the two men sitting at a table outside the coffee shop on the corner across the street. They were both wearing suits, and their bodies seemed too heavy for the thin wooden chairs. Their eyes focused sharply on the backgammon board between them. The dice flew from their hands as they rolled one play after the next. Their fingers, thin and nimble, unlike their bodies, jumped the pieces from one point to the other. The hustle and bustle of downtown Cairo didn't distract their concentration. Their game had attracted several onlookers, other men whose attention was drawn to the heightening competition. From across the street, I could catch their expletives as each move was made. I squinted through the heavy sunlight and strained my ears to hear the sounds of the dice. "Acey deucey," someone shouted, announcing the one and two that had just been rolled. It seemed that one man was just about to win when the other caught one of his pieces and sent it back to the beginning of the board.

I imagined myself crossing the street and joining the crowd to add my voice to the escalating game. The winner of the game would turn to me and ask me to play. I could hear the roll of the dice bounce against the wooden board, each throw a chance to move forward and to avoid the risk of getting trapped by my opponent. My own fingers would fly, carrying the pieces across the board, startling the audience with my quick-witted moves. The crowd would hush as I rolled the dice, and each time, I would make a move that would leave me protected and my enemy blocked on all sides. My fingers would travel the board as deftly as my grandmother's hands traveled the piano. And just when it looked like the other player would win, I would roll a double six and surpass him to win the game and hear the shouting praise of the crowd.

"Let's go, Nada," my mother said, turning her attention to me.

The salesperson had come out with my mother's purchase. He was a young man, obviously eager to please, bowing as he offered her the wrapped package of material. She accepted it and slipped a folded fifty-piaster tip into his open palm.

I succumbed to the pull of my mother's hand and turned my gaze away from the game, following her to the next store.

"You don't want to do that," my Aunt Amina said as I reached to move the black piece in the seventh row.

I pulled back my hand, stared at the backgammon board for a minute, then reached for another piece. I glanced at her. She said nothing, and her face was blank so I moved it.

I was spending the afternoon with my aunt, my mother preferring to do her shopping alone this time. Once again, I had talked my aunt into playing "just one game" with me.

"I have to cook the *molekhia* and clean before your uncle comes home," she said, trying to excuse herself.

I pleaded and she finally agreed. We settled the old wooden backgammon board on one end of the dining-room table, taking our usual places. We both knew one game would lead to another. My aunt was an expert player who knew all the tricks of the game: where to position your pieces so it was difficult for your opponent to move, how to keep them safe so they wouldn't be captured, how to move so the other person didn't block you, and how to regain your lead if you did get blocked. She even knew how to pinch the dice between your fingers to get the roll you wanted. But that trick eluded me, my fingers still not quite nimble enough to master it.

I must have been really young when my Aunt Amina started teaching me how to play backgammon, because now at the age of eleven, I considered myself almost an expert. I could play regular backgammon, *mahboosa,* and acey deuceyAnd I could roll the dice smoothly and move my pieces quickly without having to count each space, except sometimes in my head quickly. Although it was my aunt who usually won, I had beaten her enough times that now our games felt like a true competition. The possibility of winning kept me begging her to play one more game. She would usually oblige but not without complaining that the laundry had to be done, the house cleaned, and dinner prepared for my uncle.

My aunt could play as well as the men who spent their afternoons in the cafes, sitting outside, betting on their skills. In the summer months, when there was no school and the afternoon heat lingered, keeping us indoors, I spent the day at my aunt's house, enticing her to yet another game. Instead of preparing the dining table for the midday meal, we would set up the backgammon board, and the heavy afternoon hours would slip by us. With a little coaxing, I could always get her to play one more game, and sometimes, she would forget about the cleaning and cooking. One night, we stayed up until two in the morning playing one game after the other. I was playing well that night and refused to relinquish the possibility of winning, until finally, she said we had to call it even.

Aunt Amina was not a blood relative. She had married one of my maternal grandmother's eight brothers. My grandmother was born in the middle of these eight boys, and it seemed her position made her lonelier than if she had been an only child. I understood her loneliness, but I envied the brothers she had to divert her parents' attention. Before me, my mother had given birth to a boy. They called him Gamil because he was so handsome, although they planned to come up with a nickname to ward off the evil eye. But nothing ever caught on, and everyone kept calling him Gamil. My mother says that's why he died, because of envy. He was only three months old, and there seemed no reason for his death, just gone, one day not breathing as he lay in his crib. It was three years later that I came, and they named me Nada, meaning "dew," something almost invisible, to keep the evil eye at a distance. I guess it worked, but after that my mother had health problems and the doctors said no more children.

The uncle who married my Aunt Amina was the third son. I knew him as the thin, handsome one who wore a black beret, making him look more French than Egyptian. He and my aunt didn't have any children. My other uncles' wives were vague figures, shadows that slipped in and out of kitchens when we went to visit, offering us plates piled with food. Each of them had three children; it seemed to be a family requirement.

I heard rumors about my aunt's miscarriage, but it was told in whispers with too many silences between the words. She never became pregnant again, and the voices that whispered made it sound like it was her fault. My aunt had sharp red hair and a squarish face with skin that stretched tightly except around her mouth and chin where there were a few loose wrinkles. I liked her red hair and broad smile. Not having children of her own made my aunt magical to me, as if she possessed a quality of power that my other aunts lacked, each of them following suit with her three children. The whispers implied pity, but I thought my aunt was the fortunate one, able to do what she wanted, having only to look after my uncle.

The rest of her time was her own, and she seemed freer than my other aunts who were strapped to their kitchens and running after their children. I wondered if maybe she didn't want to have any children.

During one of our backgammon games, as I shook the dice in my hand, getting ready to roll, I ventured to ask her why she had never had any children after the miscarriage. She looked at me, her red hair framing her face, and the green in her eyes highlighted by the stream of sun coming through the window. "It just wasn't meant to be," she answered. I sensed that was all the answer she was willing to give, so I released the dice from my hand.

The table was set with multiple desserts—petit fours that my mother had made, *mille-feuilles,* and other pastries circling around the cake from *Groppi.* It was a round chocolate cake decorated with white roses and twirls of chocolate. It was my twelfth birthday, and we were celebrating with family coming over.

I had been looking forward to it until a few weeks ago when I began to hear my parents' mutterings about having me change schools. I was attending the Ramses School for Girls, an English-language school, where I was content and doing well. A few weeks ago, after my uncle came over with his daughter who was a few years older than me, the mutterings began. My cousin had just started attending the new French school that opened, and she came dressed in a frilly skirt and leather shoes. I was wearing my favorite stirrup pants ready to go outside, but she only wanted to play with the dolls and tea sets I kept under the bed. I was used to playing with my male cousins, joining them in their street soccer games and outdoor escapades.

Now it seemed my parents wanted to switch me to the French school. I heard their voices in the evening when they thought I was asleep. "Too much boys . . . running outside . . . that backgammon board . . . learn to be a young lady."

I came downstairs for my party wearing one of the dresses my mother had made for me. It was pale blue with a ruffled skirt fluffed out with tulle that scratched at my legs. I stayed indoors and talked to my aunts and uncles, resisting the urge to escape outside with my cousins. When it was time to blow out the candles, I stood at the side of the table, trying not to lean in too much, and I was careful to blow gently at the twelve candles, which fluttered and hesitated at the small breath I gave them. My cousin Farid leaned in over me and gave one powerful blow that extinguished all of them at once. Everyone clapped and cheered. I succeeded in avoiding the possible consequences of the French school, and my parents kept me where I was.

I made my way through the obstacles of the street, holding my elbows slightly out to block the young men from bumping against me or trying to pinch me. I had no choice but to walk that day. At three o'clock, people were going home for their midday meal, so the traffic was almost at a standstill. Neither taking a taxi nor a minibus would've gotten me there any faster. I almost tripped over a woman perched on the sidewalk who was selling matches and Chiclets. I dropped a few coins in her palm to express my remorse, then finally made my way to Groppi and pushed open the doors to enter.

I walked toward the back room of the pastry shop where a number of small round tables were set up. Farid was at one of the corner tables, and I heard his voice as I approached him. "Happy Birthday, Nada. You look beautiful," he said, standing up to greet me.

"Thank you, Farid," I responded as I sat down, releasing the weight of the street from my body. I looked up at his hazel eyes that sometimes turned to green, their color always uncertain.

"You know, in America they consider you an adult when you turn eighteen. Here, we have to wait until twenty-one," he said, leaning back and waving to catch a waiter's attention.

I smiled. Farid had a fascination with the West and was fond of making such comparisons.

"Well," I responded, "In Egypt, I don't think our parents ever consider us to be adults."

The waiter approached, and Farid ordered a Turkish coffee and a piece of *konafa* filled with sweet cream. I asked for a cup of tea and then hesitated a moment before adding the gelato. It seemed safest. The Egyptian pastries were too dense, falling heavily in my stomach, and the creamy French pastries were too sweet, keeping me thirsty for the rest of the day. At least the gelato with its icy coldness would relieve the day's heat.

"You have beautiful eyes," Farid said, paying me the standard compliment of most Egyptian men.

"Thank you," I said, not wanting to add anything that would invite another compliment.

"How's school?" he asked, leaning forward, "You'll be taking your *thanawiya amma* exams at the end of term."

"It's fine." I gave him the required answer and searched for something to turn the conversation around. "What about you? Is this your last year of medical school?" I asked, although I knew the answer. Despite not having seen each other for a while because his family had moved to Alexandria to escape the growing chaos of Cairo, my family kept up with all the gossip and news of even the most distant cousins like Farid.

"I'm doing my residency now, in anesthesiology. I'll be glad to finish so I can begin my life. What program are you hoping to enter in college?"

"My parents want me to study medicine. It's what they've always wanted," I said, shifting my body slightly away from the small table.

"You're smart; I'm sure your exam scores will get you admitted," he said.

"I'm not sure what I want," I responded, bringing the cup of tea to my lips then realizing it was still too hot.

"Well, do you want to get married?" he asked, as if he had pulled the possibility out of a hat.

I swallowed a sip of the hot tea. "God willing," I answered, giving him the customary response.

He laughed, as if I had uttered some lighthearted joke. "Oh, I'm sure God is willing but what about you?" he seemed to retaliate.

His answer took me by surprise. Usually it was my older aunts who asked me about marriage, and they were satisfied with my customary answer, interpreting it as a yes. "I don't know," I mumbled, scanning the restaurant for the waiter so I could ask for the check.

"Well, do you want children?" His questions were persistent as if he had a script to follow.

Fishing for an answer, I replied, "Actually, if I go to medical school, I'd like to specialize in pediatrics." I gave up on finding the waiter and turned to face Farid.

He let out a loud chuckle that seemed to make the table between us tremble. "Those would be other people's children, Nada. What about your own?"

I was taken aback by his laugh. Farid and I had played together as children, but we had drifted apart when his family moved to Alexandria. He had called a few days ago, saying he would be in Cairo and would like to get together. I had expected we would reminisce about our childhood, not that he would interrogate my plans for the future.

"I guess I'll want children when I'm ready," I said in a monotone, hoping my answer would appease him.

"And when will that be?" Farid prodded, continuing his interrogation.

"When . . . when I'm done with college," I replied.

"That will take a long time," Farid stated as if he were pointing out the answer to a complicated algebra problem.

I looked at my watch without any pretense of hiding it then shuffled my belongings together as I spoke. "I'm sorry, Farid, but my parents are expecting me so I really need to go. It's been nice to see you," I said, walking away before he could respond.

Outside, the hot air smacking against my face was a welcome relief from the confinement of the restaurant. Even the leering men, offering up indelicate compliments and telling me I'd make some man lucky, were preferable to Farid's questioning. I didn't know what he was after, but I didn't have it.

The answer came just a few weeks later. At breakfast, my father said, "So Nada, what are you thinking about your future?" My father's tone of voice made his question sound more like a concluding statement.

"Right now, I just want to study and do well on my final exams," I replied.

"Of course, of course," he said, "But what else, Nada?" He paused. "You're a young woman now. You need to think about marriage. Don't you want to have children?"

"Yes," I said, pushing my plate away. "One day, I do."

"Good, good," he said, as if I had just given the correct answer on a test. "Well, you're young and healthy now. You can't put it off for too long you know."

A small laugh escaped my lips, but it only sounded like a cough. "Surely it can wait until I finish college. You said you wanted me to become a doctor." I was surprised at my own words, having always avoided their conversations about my expected career. Becoming a doctor was the dream they had held for my brother, and when he died, it seemed to transfer to me, an expectation that was stamped on me at my birth.

My mother put down her fork and looked straight at me. "Nada, Farid has asked for your hand in marriage."

I swallowed my mother's words. Now Farid's insistence on

our meeting at Groppi, as well as his interrogation made sense. I had never thought of him as anything except one of the cousins in the family.

"Farid said he has spoken to you." My mother added as if this implied that I had already accepted.

Was our meeting at Groppi Farid's idea of a proposal? I tried to recollect his words but could only remember his posture, the way he slid back in the chair, already holding the superior attitude of so many doctors.

My parents waited through my silence until my father spoke again. "Nada, if your marks allow you to go to medical school, we will let you wait perhaps a year to get established in your studies; then we can have a long engagement and you can get married a year or two later. If you're not accepted into medical school, there will be no reason to wait."

My father got up after that, and my mother proceeded to collect the breakfast dishes. I was left alone at the table with only the sound of a few birds on the balcony to break the silence.

≈

The dreams began sporadically with images that flipped through my mind as I slept: a pair of dice rolling out of unseen hands—a backgammon set laid out neatly on a table ready to be played—the rows blurring together so you couldn't count them and make a move—a piece blocked by five other pieces. Then the images begin to string together and I'm walking down a small side street in Cairo. I hear the dice slapping across the wood before I see the two men at the corner café playing the game. They take turns shaking the dice with urgency then move their pieces quickly. My own inadequacy weighs heavy in my stomach, knowing my skill is no match against these players, yet my hands itch with the possibility of throwing the dice. I startle when one of the men—the heavier one with graying hair wearing a frayed brown suit, the winner of the game—asks me to play. My head barely nods. "Then sit down and play," he orders. My body is pushed toward the precarious wooden chair, and before I can sit down, the dice roll out of my hands. Sometimes the dream slows down and the weight of each move comes in slow motion, my brain sluggish as I lift the pieces. "Quicker, quicker," the man says, "count by sight." And his own hands move the pieces with the speed of a bird swooping down to its prey. I can't keep up and have to slowly count the columns to make sure. Other times, the pieces move of their own will, and I have to race after them keeping track of their rapid speed. I always wake before there is a winner, my body on the edge of the bed, about to fall off.

"Are you hungry? I have some fava beans, some cheese, or would you like some jam?"

"No, thank you," I replied to my aunt's attempt to feed me. It was Friday morning, and the previous evening I had told my parents that my aunt needed my help, so I would be spending the day with her. It was the easiest way to get out of the house and place myself in a safer position.

My aunt returned to the kitchen although I expected the offer of food would be made again. I was left sitting at the dining room table with a large jar of orange lentils and a plate on which to sort through them. I poured a good handful on the plate and began the process of picking through to find tiny pebbles or anything else that would contaminate the soup my aunt would make later that day. I pulled my long hair back into a ponytail so I could see more clearly.

Since the conversation with my parents, I had continued the motions of my life, but I knew that the movements I was making were no longer in my own hands. As I made a path through the lentils on the plate, I wondered what choices I could make. If I sat for the *thanawiya amma* exams and received sufficiently high marks, I would enter medical school, postponing for a while the decision about Farid's proposal. But I would be studying medicine, and I wasn't sure I wanted to be a doctor. If my marks were too low, the pressure to marry Farid would be difficult to resist and that meant I wouldn't attend college at all. In less than two years, I might be sitting at a table like this, sorting lentils to make dinner for my own husband, and probably pregnant. My palms began to sweat, the lentils sticking to them and slowing my progress. I tried to envision myself in bed sick with some mysterious ailment on the day of the exams. But even in my imagination, the melodrama of the scene led to nothing.

"Enough," my Aunt said, approaching me with a tray. "So what if there are stones in the lentils?" She pushed aside the plate and jar I was working through. "It's time for a cup of tea and someone has to help me eat these cookies I made." She placed the tray on the table then walked away and came back with the backgammon set. "How about a game?" Before I could answer, she added, "Let's play *mahboosa*—we haven't played that in a long time."

Mahboosa was one of the riskiest games, and as a child, I didn't like playing it because I never seemed to have a chance of winning. If you had only one piece on a triangle, and the other player landed on the same spot, they didn't just send your piece back to the beginning to start all over, instead they kept their piece on top of yours, making it impossible for you to move. That one piece could remain stuck until the other player finally decided to move their own piece.

The afternoon began to seep in with its heavy light, and outside, the city quieted down for its siesta, only an occasional shout or taxi horn punctuating the silence. We played one game after the next, my aunt guiding me through the moves as I figured out new maneuvers to make my way through the game.

I sat at the edge of my bed with my back straight, the awkwardness of my posture helping me to resist the desire to slip under the covers. The conversation had not gone as I had planned that evening. Just as my father was about to get up after finishing his meal, I broached the subject. My first mistake was beginning by saying, "I have made a decision." Perhaps if I had begun by requesting their approval, things might have gone better. Then I let the words tumble out, trying to say it all in one sentence: applying to schools in America . . . getting an acceptance along with a scholarship . . . going . . . not taking the end of the year exams. My father's glare evolved into screaming, and I couldn't catch his sentences, only the repetition of "who makes the decision?" My mother's silence felt louder, her face marking her inevitable loss. Cornered, I shouted back at my father, "If my brother had lived and been accepted into an American college, would you have let him go?" As soon as the words fell, I wished I could have gathered them back up. But it was too late, and, in silence, we all retreated to separate spaces in the house.

I heard a slight knock followed by the door creaking open. My parents stood at the entrance of the room. I hadn't turned on the light and their silhouettes appeared like shadows in the door frame.

"You can go," my father said, the effort of his words apparent.

"You have our blessing," my mother added, inhaling her grief.

I could only utter a useless "thank you."

They turned around, and I was left alone still sitting on the edge of the bed. Everything in my room felt alien, as if already I didn't belong here. I would pack my suitcases, small artifacts to take with me into a new world I could not imagine.

EARLY ARRIVAL

Phone Call Two

Aloo—Aloo—mama—*Aloo—ezayek ya mama* how are you mama—yes, we're well—*kol sana we entee tayeba* Happy Easter—did you go to church last night—no, there isn't a church here yet—yes yes, we are all well—*ezay baba* how is dad—how is his health—and is my sister well—yes, my daughter is fine and her English has become much better—and is my uncle well—why what's wrong—but he's going to be well—*ensha allah* god willing—give him my greetings—*kol sana we entoo tayebeen* Happy Easter to all of you—yes, here they celebrated last month in March but we are celebrating today with you—we will eat lamb—no, I didn't make *kahek* this year—I miss you mama—I wish we could be with you today—and are you well mama—what time is it over there?—they turned the time back so now it's six hours difference—here it is seven in the morning—yes, the phone lines were open—I miss you mama—*ma elsalama—ma elsalama*

The Top

Light filtered through the thin slats of the closed window blind, creating a pattern of long, narrow stairs on the opposite wall. Shoukry stared at it as he sat at the round linoleum-topped kitchen table waiting for his wife to bring him a cup of coffee and some toast. The pattern shifted with the direction of the light until it started to fade and his eyes lost its movement.

Walking quickly toward him, his wife set down the demitasse of Arabic coffee and a plate with two pieces of toast sliding back and forth precariously. "Here," she said, barely parting her lips. Before he could ask about butter, she had bustled away. He sipped the coffee and ate the toast as it was, occasionally glancing up at the wall to see if the pattern might return in a different form.

"I have to go in early today," she said, grabbing her pocketbook and sweater. "If you come home before me, there is hamburger in the refrigerator. You can put it in the oven."

"Amira, what about Amira?" he asked.

"She has a meeting after school."

The desk in his office in Egypt had been very large. Even if he bent forward and stretched his arms to either side as far as he could, feeling the tendons on the inside of his elbows pull and strain, his fingertips would barely grip the edges. The desk chair was cushioned, and it twirled around. The men who came to see him sat on a straight-backed hard wooden chair. They would lean forward, their hands vigorously explaining their request. He would relax, fit his body into the chair's contoured shape and let it rock a little with his movements. Never would he move his body closer to the man in front of him. Even when shaking hands, he would stand upright behind his desk, so the other man had to bend forward to reach his hand. It was this precision of his movements, he believed, that had earned him the respect of his colleagues and the men who came to see him. That was why he was called Ustaz and Pasha.

He was in charge of issuing permits for the construction of new apartment buildings or adding more floors to old ones. With the population growing so fast and so many enterprising young men eager to gain some of the profit, his office had a long list of appointments that stretched six months ahead. About once every month, he would refuse to give a permit because the new government building codes had not been followed. The rest of the time, he might overlook certain discrepancies if he were offered some compensation in return. He would debate with the man across from him that the codes were really too strict given the rising cost of building materials. In his mind, he justified his actions by convincing himself that he was adhering to a set of revised codes based on his own better judgment. He thoroughly enjoyed discussing the building projects with the builders and felt himself to be an expert, often giving advice on the drawings laid out for him.

"And why not? Are we less than anyone?"

"I said no. Our lives here are good and we will stay here."

"Why don't you look around you? Everyone wants to leave this country and its misery."

"What misery? I've reached a high position in my work. And here we are living in an apartment that is beautiful and large. What more do you want?"

"I want what all people want. I want a house for myself with a garden and a fancy car. I want to go out to enjoy myself and to see the world. I want my freedom, not this society that suffocates our desires."

"The world is in your home in front of you, your husband and your daughter. We are your world."

"You're just afraid. A coward."

"That's enough. You've given me a headache."

"Look at my sister's husband. He doesn't even have a college degree like you. And they've only been in America for six months, and now they have a house and a car. Think. You, with your college degree and your experience, how far you can go in America! This is a country that gives opportunities that one can't imagine."

"Enough. Enough. Just what do you want from me?"

"At least think about it, Shoukry. Lots of people are emigrating now, especially after the '67 war. And all of them, in a short while, achieve a high position, and they have things we can never reach here even if we work till we die. This country is closed. Abd el Nasser doesn't want to let anything in. And he's fighting everyone's battles. Everything that is of worth in the country he lets go. There's no future here."

"Let's thank God for what we have and not look too far. My work is good. There is no need."

"If we were going to America, think how people would see you. They would look at you as if you were a king. This America is heaven."

"All right. All right."

"Will you think about it?"

"Yes. Yes."

"Why don't you get the application tomorrow from the embassy? We can just look at it. We won't lose anything."

Fifth floor, please.
Ninth floor, please.
Tenth floor.
Top floor, please.
Good morning, Sir.
Good afternoon, Miss.
How are you today, Shoukry, the fifteenth floor.

Like a continuous circle but flat, never curving out, no interior space inside the lines. Confined in this elevator, pushing buttons, taking people up, down. The high metal stool to lean against, occasionally rest the weight of the body, back stiff, supported by a thin slip of air. Surrounded by tongues inside lips dancing out sounds that merged into a flat rhythm, repetition of *th*. Alone, pressing tongue between teeth into a windblown whistle.

And his wife, *his* wife. She didn't even have a college degree. Now working in an office with her own desk. Thinking she's somebody. Lying, lying to everyone. Making it all up. Filling out the application with her sister at her shoulder instructing. Say you graduated from Cairo University. Tell them you worked at the National Egyptian Insurance Company. They won't know. They can't check. Put an x next to filing. It's easy, just putting things in order by letter. You'll get the job.

Interviews. Straining to determine when the word ends and another begins. The sentence stopping. His turn to speak. Lips in jigsaw pieces to form the shape for the word to pull it out.

Then she says, "I got you a job. You'll be in charge. Practically your own boss."

≈

"Where's Amira?"

"A friend picked her up early this morning. She's going on a weekend ski trip with her school."

"And why wasn't I told? Don't you need my permission? I'm her father."

"I signed the permission slip for her. You were asleep and she had to take it in that day."

"And did you find out anything about this trip? Are there boys going too? Don't you think about your daughter's reputation? You want her to ruin herself?

"Oh Shoukry, calm down. It's a school trip. Don't make a fuss over nothing."

In the elevator, sometimes, the smell of flour, bread, the baking of crust, would whisper through his nose. He'd twirl his tongue around the crevices of his mouth searching for the taste of that holy bread, the *orban* he ate as a child. Going to church with his parents in Coptic Cairo, walking through the cobblestone alleyways to the Hanging Church where his father was a chanter. At the end of the liturgy, the smell of incense swung from the priest's gold chalice as he walked down the aisles between the rows of pews. The smoke would flood Shoukry's nostrils and mix with the floury smell of the *orban* just being brought out.

On the way home from church, women placed themselves throughout the alleyway with baskets of holy bread for sale. Dressed in sheer layers of black that became opaque, each one enticed him with her song. He would beg his mother for a piaster to buy his very own *orban,* round and whole with the pattern of crosses engraved in its center, instead of just that small bite the priest handed out. Only on holidays would she give him the piaster, and he would eat the bread slowly and possessively, trying to redesign the crosses with each bit that he tore off to put in his mouth.

But in the elevator this craving came over him like a shadow until he was sure that if he could only trail the smell he would find the *orban.* Sometimes when the elevator door opened, he would stick out his face and sniff, trying to catch the direction of it. But people would rush in too quickly and he would lose its trace. Once, he was concentrating so hard, the door almost closed on his nose, and he heard the echo of laughter around him. Still, he would creep his tongue over his lips in hopes of catching a hint of its taste.

"Shoukry, you look a little tired. Why don't you go home early today?"

The house was quiet. For a while, he sat on the sofa and waited for his wife to return. When he got hungry, he went to the refrigerator. Leaning against the door, he looked inside. A little milk on the top shelf, an almost empty jar of mayonnaise in the door and, on the middle shelf, an eggplant. It had a long neck then it curved out, smooth and round. All of it was a deep layered shade of purple. "Too big to make stuffed eggplant," he thought. Just then he heard the key in the lock and quickly closed the refrigerator door and returned to the sofa.

His wife and daughter entered with bags of groceries. He could see that his wife had a beaming smile on her face.

"When will you start?" he overheard his daughter asking.

"In two weeks. I'll be the supervisor of my own department, and I'm going to have my own office. They're giving me a very good raise."

His wife turned to him as she put the last of the groceries away. "Well, Shoukry, aren't you glad? I got promoted today."

In the dream, he was a young boy just coming out of the church. The sun was hazy that day, relieving the usual heavy heat of the summer months. It must have been after his father died since his mother was wearing black. She was talking to one of his aunts, and they walked together ahead of him. While kicking a small stone and following its path, he spotted the round worn piaster. Just as he picked it up, he saw a woman selling the bread and went toward her, stretching out his hand with the coin. Smiling, the woman handed him the bread and spoke some words of blessing. He heard his mother calling and began to run. While running, he looked down to see the *orban*, but his hands clutched only air. He woke with a small scream stuck in his throat. Still expecting to see the bread, he looked but found nothing except his fingers in the same position as in the dream.

≈

It was after having the dream that it became difficult for him to press the elevator buttons with his right hand. He would reach for them, but his fingers refused to separate, and his arm wanted to remain secured to his side. Now he had to turn his body slightly sideways so he could press with his left hand.

"How are you feeling, Shoukry? Maybe you should see a doctor. You don't look too well."

People's stares began to bother him, and sometimes he would begin to explain about the craving, about how the *orban* had disappeared. But before he could seek out all the words, the person would get off the elevator, leaving his words half-formed.

≈

One day, another craving came over him. Strong and overpowering like the smell of vinegar, the taste of *koshari* settled on his lips. His mother would make it during Lent when they could only eat what didn't come from an animal. Rice, lentils, and pasta with a few chickpeas and the spiced, almost tart tomato sauce, but most of all the thin, crisp-fried onions he always demanded more of. The taste kept scratching at his mouth until he almost went frantic stretching his tongue for it.

It had to be here, somewhere close. If only he could get out of the elevator, he would find it.

The beeps calling the elevator down stung at his ears, but he kept going up, up to the very top where the tourists went, in one movement that felt like could be flying, until finally the elevator stopped flat with a drop. He put the key in to keep the door open and stepped out.

The sun's brightness flooded his eyes and he squinted sharply to be able to see. A gust of wind came around him, and he smelled dust and heat, but no *koshari*. He sniffed harder, but the smell was gone. He walked to the railing and looked over the Boston skyline, buildings sprouting out of the ground as if they were ancient trees. He wondered at the elevators in these buildings, if all of them had someone like him who pressed their buttons and ran them through the length of the day. His eyes focused again on the breadth of the landscape, and he began to walk around, keeping his head turned to see the city revolving.

When he had made a full circle and returned to his original spot by the railing, he could hear buzzing and hard pounding coming up from the elevator. The banging increased in his ears. There was the elevator standing with its door open. He stared at it then looked around and saw the neon EXIT sign next to it. He opened the door and began to descend the stairs. His feet were sluggish, but as the spiral continued, he gained speed and a rhythm guided his feet down till it became a repetitive tapping. He held the railing with his left hand and felt the smoothness of it slide against his palm. Soon there was only a swirl of white from the walls and the tapping as he wound around, unhinged, from the ground all the way down.

A large crowd of people had gathered, including at least two groups of tourists. His head was still going around, and it was difficult to keep his feet still once he was standing in one spot. He saw a man hurrying toward him, his face red and his arms gesticulating wildly. He must calm him down, he thought.

"It's all right, Mahmoud. Don't worry. I'll put the paperwork through, and you'll be able to build those apartments in no time. Just be a little patient. There's no need . . ."

But the man was now shaking him and screaming, "You bastard, you foreign idiot! What do you think you're doing? Going up there for a breath of fresh air! Where the hell is the elevator? What do you think this is, an amusement park?"

Shoukry tried to understand, to answer him, until a woman came up and began to pull the man back.

"Stop shaking him," she said. "Can't you see he's crazy? He's not even speaking English."

The First Lesson

She opened the oven door, her thumb and four fingers working awkwardly in the thick glove meant to protect her from the heat. With her free hand, she tugged at the aluminum foil until it uncovered the roast beef. It sizzled, surrounded by a mosaic of small red potatoes, diagonally cut carrots, and pearl onions. She pulled off the foil to let the beef brown then closed the oven door, relieved to feel the fire draining from her face and to loosen her hand from the glove. She looked up at the round clock framed in a red circle. Ten to five. Only ten minutes to finish the salad and get dressed. Well, surely they wouldn't be here at exactly five; guests always arrived at least fifteen minutes late. She mixed the salad hurriedly, trying to catch the lettuce leaves and tomatoes that kept getting tossed over the bowl's rim. Then she returned to the oven, opening it quickly so that the smoke leaped out at her, forcing her to straighten her back and blink several times before she could see well enough to lift the heavy pan out. The roast beef had browned and looked almost crispy. It's just right, she thought, pulling it out of the oven and replacing the aluminum foil over it.

"I'm going to go up to get dressed," she shouted toward the open basement door.

"OK," came her husband's reply, sounding only like a soft hum by the time it climbed the stairs.

"Are you done or not yet?"

"Almost, I'm wiping the glasses."

At five o'clock, the doorbell rang. It's impossible, Nagwa

thought, as she settled the blue dress gently over her head to avoid getting any makeup on its collar. But then she heard the greetings exchanged between her husband and the neighbors. Picking up the blue belt, she stretched its thick elastic around her waist and brought the buckle together. It pushed into the middle of her body, catching her breath for a moment. Lifting her face to the mirror, she ran her fingers through the edges of her black hair around her neck to make it look fuller. She had been trying to lose weight, but her body still appeared rounded, drawn out curves that held her weight to the ground. She felt her collarbone. Yes, if she lost enough weight, she could have angles like the models she saw in the magazines. She straightened the dress around the belt, practiced a silent smile and hello into the mirror then went down the stairs.

Betty and Michael were seated on the light blue velvet couch next to each other. Her husband was sitting upright in the black recliner across from them.

"Hello," Nagwa said as she approached them.

"Hi, Nagwa," they both seemed to say at once.

Nagwa didn't realize that they hadn't stood up to shake hands until she was practically standing right in front of them. She heard a soft chuckle as Michael got up and reached for her hand. Michael was almost six feet with firm shoulders that seemed to hold still even when he was walking. Nagwa's smile wavered as she stared into his face, almost forgetting to put any pressure into the handshake. She smiled more easily when she turned to Betty's soft brown eyes and lighter handshake. Betty's brown hair was short and curled in neatly at the nape of her neck, and she had a slim figure that seemed to move with the same ease as a branch in the wind.

"How are you?" asked Betty, turning toward Nagwa who sat down on the further end of the couch.

"I'm fine. Thank you."

"Where's your daughter?"

"Oh, she's watching TV. Let me go get her."

Nagwa got up but felt suddenly conscious of having to pass by the two of them. Turning toward her husband, she whispered in Arabic, "Ask them if they want to drink something."

She opened the door to what they referred to as "the family room," since that's what the real-estate agent had called it. Her daughter, ten years old, was sitting cross-legged on the couch with a blank stare toward the TV. Her long, dark hair was tied back in a ponytail. They had argued over what she should wear, finally settling on a pair of brown corduroy pants and a blue shirt with a lace collar.

"Get up," Nagwa said, "the guests are here, and it's improper not to greet them."

"I'll come in a minute, Mom," her daughter replied, not turning her head away from the TV.

"Now," Nagwa said as she took two quick strides toward the TV and turned it off.

Her daughter uttered a heavy sigh and followed her into the living room. She said hello, shook hands, then sat on a chair in the corner.

The conversation centered on the neighborhood, with Betty and Michael mostly filling them in on all the neighbors. It was a quiet suburban street with every house designed as a Cape Cod, the slanting roofs deceptively camouflaging the second floor. Each family differentiated their house by color so that the street resembled a line of miniature-block constructions.

Nagwa and her husband had moved into their house about six months ago, and Betty had come over shortly afterwards with some banana bread to say hello and welcome them to the neighborhood. Nagwa was so pleased that she immediately started making plans to invite them over for dinner. It was the first time that Americans had come to their house. She hadn't wanted to invite anyone until they bought their own home. The apartment they had lived in for the first year was too small.

This house was not exactly what she had planned, but it would be better once she fixed up the upstairs. They would move their bedroom up there. The room would be large enough for their furniture as well as two chairs and a small table where they could have coffee in the morning. Maybe she could knock part of the wall out and put in a large curved window like the one she had seen in *Better Homes,* folding the corner of the page to save it. Besides, they wouldn't live here permanently. She was sure they would eventually buy a larger house in a nicer area. For a moment, she pictured the mansion she had seen in the last movie before leaving Egypt, set on a hill surrounded by an even landscape of grass. It had two garages with a Jaguar parked in front.

Betty was going on about some of the restaurants in the area, which made Nagwa remember dinner. Excusing herself, she went to the kitchen. After the table was set, she began arranging the food on serving platters. Once everything was on the table, she stepped back to look. It was only an eating area separated from the kitchen by a counter. They had bought a round white Formica table with four red vinyl chairs. It was the best she could find that would fit into the area. A more formal table would have looked out of place in the kitchen.

Her dining room in Egypt had an exquisite oval table where twelve people could comfortably place themselves. The glass top reflected the cherry wood underneath, stained lightly to the color of a hazelnut. In the store, she and her mother had pulled at each other's nerves, her mother insisting that she must impress people with furniture built heavy to the ground, holding its darkness like a ripe date. But Nagwa's eyes kept moving to the curve of the table's soft lines that seemed to flow like the boats on the Nile with their sails folding into the wind. Realizing she would not be the victor in this battle, Nagwa made a bid for a compromise: she would agree to the traditionally elaborate bedroom set her mother had chosen if she could get this more modern dining room.

All the furniture had to be sold before they left the country. Relatives, friends, and strangers had landed in their house, surveying it like an excavation site. The dining room was one of the first things sold at a fraction of its original cost. The day it was being moved, Nagwa had purposely gone downtown, claiming she urgently needed some shoes for the trip.

Blinking her eyes, Nagwa focused on the table in front of her. She refolded a napkin then stepped into the living room.

The conversation had turned to property taxes and the increasing cost of houses. She waited for their tones to slide into quietness; then she announced that dinner was ready. They turned to her voice and rose to go into the kitchen. Moving around the table, they each chose a seat cautiously as her husband got an extra chair for their daughter and made sure everyone had their drinks. Once they were all seated, Nagwa whispered to her husband that he should cut the meat. He had to step between Betty and Nagwa to plug the electric knife in and position himself so he could reach the roast beef easily. The knife hummed a staccato rhythm as he lightly seesawed into the meat, trying to be careful not to shred it, as his wife had warned him earlier. Having cut about half of it, he straightened himself and mumbled that he could cut more later.

"Please, help yourself," Nagwa said as she passed the vegetables to Betty. She made sure each dish made it around the table, her eyes traveling from one plate to the next to ensure that each held a portion of every item.

"I hope you like it," Nagwa suggested as they started eating.

"Everything is delicious," replied Betty, as she lifted her smile toward Nagwa.

Their eating was interrupted by some brief comments about the weather and the best way to dress during the cold. As Nagwa glanced toward Betty and Michael's plates, she noticed that each of them had only taken one or two bites out of the meat and were concentrating on the vegetables and salad. Her own appetite stalled. Her husband and daughter were eating well, and she saw her husband getting ready to reach for another piece of the roast beef. She had cooked it the same way she always did, just as she had learned from her mother who had a reputation for being the best cook in the family. In the past, everyone who ate it commented on how well it tasted.

She turned to Michael, "Michael, please, would you like another piece of meat?"

"Oh, no, I'm getting quite full," he replied bringing the napkin to the corner of his mouth.

Nagwa swallowed, taking her breath in, "Is there anything wrong? Don't you like the food?"

Betty and Michael raised their heads. She saw Betty about to speak, but she heard Michael's voice saying, "Do you really want the truth?"

"Oh, yes, of course, please tell me."

Her husband and daughter held their forks still as they looked up.

"Well," Michael said, breathing out and straightening his body against the back of the chair, "I'll be honest with you. You had a very good piece of meat here, but you ruined it by over cooking it. It's practically burned."

Nagwa's features fell like a stage curtain closing.

Michael wiped his hands on the napkin and placed it by his plate. "Meat should be cooked so it's still pink inside. You want the meat to be tender, not tough."

Nagwa raised her face to meet Michael's eyes. "I see," she said, "Thank you. Thank you for telling me. I appreciate it. Now I have learned something."

It appeared that dinner was over, so they returned to the living room. Nagwa brought out the tea and a crème caramel dessert. When it was time for her guests to leave, Nagwa thanked Michael again and promised them another better cooked dinner.

Nagwa returned to the kitchen to clean up while her husband and daughter brought in the cups and dishes from the living room. She picked up the plate with the remaining roast beef and placed it on the counter. Bringing out the aluminum foil, she rolled out a piece and cut it along the sharp edge of the box. As she was about to place it over the meat, she looked down. He's right, she thought, it is burned, but now I have learned something. She wrapped the foil around the meat, walked over to the trash can by the refrigerator, pressed her foot on the lever so that the cover came up, and threw in the wrapped package.

Playground

She had learned the way to school, a footstep pattern she recorded and repeated. Each morning, out the door, turn right, toward the hand you eat with, to the end of the street, then another right to the school building. And come back the same way, taking opposite turns. But at the end of the street, she would stop, uncertain if she had gone too far. She strained to see the school building, but the corner house blocked everything beyond it. She made the turn hesitantly, slowing till she caught sight of the large field, the swings, the school, then drew a breath of courage that lengthened her steps. On the way back, right and left reversed, distracting her eyes. The dark brown house on the other side made her look back to trace the path she had taken, to consider if she had crossed a street without realizing it, and decide if she must return and cross back.

But when the boys began chasing her, she had to make quicker decisions, risk the turn in the road rather than stop and take on the attack. She ran faster, sometimes out-running them and got into the house before their hands could reach her. At dismissal, she learned to edge her way to the far end of the schoolyard, right up to the corner fence, and her ears could detect the second before the bell to give herself a head start. When their heads turned to look for her, she was already gone, running close to the houses, scraping her shoulder against wooden fences to remain out of sight.

She had arrived in a child's body, dressed in a wool dress that itched at her skin and black leather shoes snug around her toes. In the first year, her body rounded into breasts and hips that strained against seams and pushed new patterns into cloth. Her period came at ten, the same age as her cousin still in Egypt, but she didn't know that. Her breasts grew large, soft mounds spilling out of thin bras.

The children's jeers hefted through the playground, carried by the sharp winds of running feet. And inside the classroom, words slipped out of thin lips and tucked themselves into cracked open desks. She held her ears silent, tried to keep the sounds from hooking under her skin. But even the girls joined in, their pink mouths unloading giggles as they asked to see, just to see what they looked like. She let them once because they said they were her friends and that she was so lucky to have them.

She unbuttoned her shirt, pinched the bra underneath with her fingers to lift it over her breasts. Their eyes grew wide as they saw brown smooth flesh ending in dark spirals and a slight nipple like a crown to some majestic mountain. Across her upper chest, the elastic stretched tight, edged into the flesh under her arms, keeping her breath shallow. Her breasts hung as if cut from some tree branch about to wither.

A few days later when winter began to sift out the warm air, the boys' groping increased. Arms stretched to squeeze, to grab, and it was hard to escape while held against a tree in the far end of the playground. Coat, mittens, hat weighed her down, and in boots zipped against calves, she couldn't run quickly enough. They caught her more often, and her chest ached from pinching and squeezing. She learned to run with elbows tucked at her sides to protect herself.

If she ran fast enough or if they grabbed at her once or twice, they would give up the chase. But once, on a heavy winter day filled with snow, they kept after her all the way home. Pinned against the side of her house, snowballs flew at her, sparks shooting cold into her eyes as the hard packed snow pounded her body. The snowballs snapped through the air, aimed from different directions. Some hit the wall, slid down to the ground. Her body couldn't dodge the others that flew like rocks from a slingshot, slapping her sides, her chest, her face, hard and solid.

It was 1971, and she sat in the second to last seat, in double rows of desks, next to a girl whose face faded behind thin strands of light brown hair that covered the corners of her eyes.

"Where are you from?"

She answered with words crumbling out of her lips like chipped china.

"Did you have a camel?"

Her brown skin unrolled like a skein of cloth.

"Did you live in a pyramid?"

Her feet pressed into green earth.

The history book lay flat. Left page, upper right corner, slipping into the edge of the open spine, a square picture: distant shot of three pyramids and in the forefront a man, head wrapped in white turban, next to a camel whose gaze turned sideways.

The boy's hair was brown, darker than the others', and his tall wiry body bent as if urged by the wind. When he asked, she let him in after school when the house was still empty, because he smiled at her and held back from the teasing. His body lay heavy over her naked breasts, their softness exposed like moss dug from moist earth. He ground his hips, an irregular rhythm, against her abdomen as he squeezed, grabbed, pinched her breasts like rubber balls. She wanted him to kiss her like the movies she glimpsed on the TV, but his head was bent, and his eyes didn't shift their gaze to her face. His mouth brushed her lips as he lifted his body to leap out the door.

Winter lengthened that year, and the snow continued to sit slippery and silent. The frozen ground slowed her to tiny steps, afraid she might get pulled down to the icy surface. The taunting and teasing carried on in the playground, increasing like the volume on the TV.

Once, finding herself surrounded during recess, she turned to her closest adversary and began kicking, hard sharp kicks at his lower leg. Her boots were solid, and her aim was instinctive. His yelp muted the others' voices as he lifted his leg and his eyes watered with pain. When another approached her, she repeated the same motion, finding pleasure in the energy that slid down her foot and the impact of hitting her target. Her ability surprised her. She watched, alarmed at discovering that she could cause pain. She had seen fights on the playground, boys tackling each other and even girls pulling hair and biting, but it had never occurred to her that she had any strength she could use.

She learned quickly. If the first kick didn't stop them, then she moved to rapid kicks, one after the other in quick succession till hitting the same spot over and over sent them away. And even if they held her arms, she could kick. Her legs kept moving, and if two boys came at her, she could kick with both feet. It was like following a beat, a drum beat that only she could hear, and no one else could catch its rhythm to stop her.

Lentils

The second morning after their arrival, Safia woke up looking for lentils. She found onions, garlic, oil, in the kitchen cabinets, and fortunately she had some cumin with her. At the last minute, while they were packing, she came across a small bag of cumin on the kitchen counter. Reluctant to throw it away, she stuck it in the corner of her suitcase, and it had passed through customs. But she needed orange lentils. Her husband's cousin, with whom they were staying, was still asleep, so there was no one to ask.

She rummaged through the few cabinets in the kitchen. Aside from several cans of vegetables and a bag of pasta, there was nothing useful. She sat at the table that wobbled as she pulled the chair to it and drank her tea. It tasted bitter despite the three spoons of sugar, and her tongue kept searching for the flavor of mint leaves. She felt a slight chill at her shoulder. Turning to face the window, she was surprised that she could see nothing through it. The glass was glazed with a layer of frost. Thinking it was on the inside, she placed her hand against it, but all she felt was the cold coming through her fingertips.

They had waited until April in order to avoid the cold weather. It would be spring by then, their friends predicted, and they wouldn't need winter coats or boots. When her husband had received notification that they had been approved for immigration, she worried about arriving in the midst of cold and snow that would stiffen their bones. But the paperwork and medical exams took some time, and she was relieved when

April was decided as the month of their departure. Now, rubbing the window with no results, she was not so sure they had outwitted the seasons.

She heard a door open and looked up to see Adel, her husband's cousin, coming out of his bedroom.

"Good morning," she said.

"Good morning," he replied, squinting his eyes to see her.

"Adel, do you have any lentils?"

He turned slightly to focus on her, "Why do you need lentils?"

"I want to make *aats*."

For a moment, he continued to stare at her. Then he turned to go to the bathroom.

After a few weeks, they found an apartment, and she was glad they could get settled in their own place. She had felt uneasy staying with Adel, but he was their only relative in America. That's why they had decided to come to Michigan, so they could at least be with family. She had wished they could have gone to California where she heard the weather was warm. But at least now she was settled in her own place. Safia had organized everything and was ready to begin the task of housekeeping. They had bought some furniture from the previous tenant, an old woman who spoke with a quick accent that made it difficult to understand exactly how much money she wanted. The apartment was on the tenth floor of a high-rise that was part of a three-building unit. They lined up facing each other, rectangular blocks rising to the sky. At first it astonished her that there was no balcony. Even the poorest of homes in Egypt had some sort of balcony, to let the air circulate through the apartment and where you could sit, drink a cup of tea, and watch the activity on the street. Sometimes if a merchant came by with a cart full of prickly pears, it was easier to let down a basket than to climb down the steps. But here the coolness of the weather made her reluctant to even open the windows, and soon she stopped walking through the streets with her head tilted up, looking for balconies. Getting used to the window shades took longer. There were no shutters to open for air and close to keep the sun and dust out. Instead, there were plastic shades with a string that would only go up halfway when pulled.

Safia was a short woman, about five feet in height, and although she was not fat, her body had filled out after two children. When her brother died several years ago, she wore black for forty days as was the custom; afterwards, it seemed difficult to return to brighter colors. Now in her early fifties, she tended to wear blues and grays. Occasionally she would buy a print but with a small design. Her black hair, which she usually wore pulled back in a kind of bun, had streaked with gray, so every few months she would mix henna and rub it through her hair. In the sun, threads of red would shine, their intensity depending on the angle of light.

The first time Safia went to a supermarket, the aisles of food astounded her, especially the apples—red, green, yellow, shiny, and whole. When she was a child, sometimes her father brought home two or three apples. They were imported and difficult to find in those days. Everyone would gather in the living room. Then her mother would cut the apples into quarters and passed them around, the white heart of the apple divided and the seeds taken out. They were so special that each quarter seemed like a whole apple. Here, as she traveled down each aisle, the colors and shapes of packages made her eyes dizzy. It took her several hours to shop as she tried to decipher each item. When she got home, she told her husband that they could buy everything in one store: there was a butcher, a fruit stall, a grocery, and a bakery all in the same place. But, as she unpacked the food, she realized that she hadn't bought the orange lentils, or some of the other things she needed. Next time she would have to look more carefully or find someone to ask.

But, no matter how much she looked or asked, she couldn't

find the lentils. There were only the brown ones that she could use to make *koshari* and some yellow ones. One day in late May, when the temperature had dipped unexpectedly into the forties, and the chill made her again desire the taste of *aats*, she desperately bought the yellow ones, hoping they would turn the right color once cooked. But the soup tasted bland, like drinking tea from a paper cup, and no matter how much salt or cumin she added, she couldn't imitate the rich sharp taste of a bowl of *aats*. After that, she gave up on the lentils, and fortunately the weather got warmer. She concentrated her efforts on finding other things.

Safia's searches led her to only a few of the items she wanted, so she tried to adjust or do without. Her greatest trouble came with the spices. The rows of jars in the supermarket convinced her she could find what she was looking for, but the names were unfamiliar and she couldn't open them to smell. After some frustration, she remembered the Arabic-English dictionary she had brought with her; it was a small, thick book with a hard green cover. She pored over it. It had been a long time since she used a dictionary, not since she was a young girl. Now she was grateful for those years of struggling with the rules of English.

Kamoon was cumin and *cosbara* was coriander; those were easy. It was the *boharat* that seemed impossible. Once, she even called her children in Egypt, hoping they could help her. Both were grown and married now; her son was a pharmacist and her daughter a tour guide. But, despite their knowledge of English, the only translation they could give her was simply "spices." Once, when she found something labeled "Allspice," it seemed hopeful. But when she mixed it with the ground meat and onions she was frying, the result was an odd sweetness that made her rub her tongue against the roof of her mouth to dissolve the taste. Without the *boharat*, many of the things she cooked had little flavor. She missed the way the

Egyptian spice delved into the food and heightened its taste so that it tingled on your tongue.

Fortunately, her husband ate and said nothing. Whenever she asked, he would simply say, "Fine. fine." She guessed he was too preoccupied to really notice. He had been an engineer in Egypt with a good job helping to design some of the new apartment buildings. The last project he worked on was a building with several two-floor apartments intended for the elite in Egypt, the foreigners, and the Gulf Arabs who came to do business or shop. But his salary had been only adequate, and he was frustrated by working with others who were paid three times as much simply because they held foreign passports. He was the one who had initiated their emigration, urging her along, promising her a better life. He assured her that if things didn't go well, they would return after they had their citizenship so he could at least have a better job in Egypt. She was content with her life and tried to convince him that they were too old to start over again, both of them over fifty, but she could see the longing in his eyes and agreed. A few weeks after they arrived, he managed to find a job, and he was pleased with the salary. He felt more settled and able to take in his new surroundings.

One evening after supper, he said, "How about making us some *baklawa?"*

"Sure," she answered, but after a pause, during which she ran down the list of ingredients in her head, she added, "Well, I'll have to find the phyllo and rose water."

Safia took herself to all the supermarkets in town until at last she found frozen packages of phyllo in one of them. It was thicker in texture than the one in Egypt, but she decided it would do. The rose water was another matter. When she asked the clerks, they would either lead her to the fresh flowers or to the flavored seltzer waters. After a few weeks, she began to worry. Her husband hadn't mentioned the baklava again, but she didn't want to disappoint him.

In Egypt, the kitchen had been Safia's domain. It was spacious with enough room for a small table in the middle where sometimes just she and her husband would have their meals. A window on the east side brought in a breeze during the afternoon that helped to ease the heat from the stove. On the counter by the window, she placed a tray with four *olas* on it. As the clay jugs formed beads of sweat on the outside that dripped onto the tray, the water inside them became cool enough to soothe their thirst in the summer. Her cabinets were filled with assorted jars. One had jams that she made when each fruit was in season: there was grape, sweet lemon, orange rind. And another cabinet held her pickled eggplant, peppers, and the sharp, tangy white cheese that she soaked in lemon and olive oil. In her family, she had a reputation for being a clever cook, and it pleased her when her work was complimented.

One day, almost a year after their arrival, Safia woke to the sun stretching an arrow across her bed. She blinked then got up and went to the window. The sun was deceptive here. After a few times of going out of the apartment with a short-sleeved dress, only to be met by the frost air pinching her arms, she had learned to be more cautious. Today, she touched the window and found it warm. Her husband was still sleeping, and she decided to go get some milk so they could have *shehria* for breakfast. At least she had found the thin vermicelli she could turn into the sweet breakfast dish.

The air was unusually calm this morning, and the warmth against her skin was pleasant. Safia walked with an even pace, each step the same length. She kept her back straight, and her chin level so that her gaze remained steady. When she was a child, she would watch her feet as she walked. Her mother kept telling her to look up until finally the lesson had taken hold.

When Safia arrived at the store, it was closed and wouldn't be open for another hour. Hesitant of what to do, she stared at the sign listing the store's hours. The milk wasn't important, but she was reluctant to return home on such an unusual morning. She made a left turn, figuring she could make a wide circle to extend the way home. A bird whistled, and Safia looked around to find it. A robin stood in the middle of the street on the concrete, its red chest puffed out and its beak open. She watched as the bird whistled another song, then flew off.

When she was young, she had been amazed at her mother's ability to know the future. She would tell her when she was going to get a present, when someone was coming to visit, when she would do well on an exam. Whenever she asked her how she knew, her mother would answer, "A little bird whispered it in my ear." The response perplexed her, and she wondered how her mother could communicate with the birds. She spent hours watching the birds in their yard, tiny and gray with quick flapping wings. It was not until she had her own children that she understood, and she too explained to their puzzled faces that a bird had whispered the secret in her ear.

Safia got lost in her thoughts, and as she focused on her surroundings again, she saw that the streets had become wider and the houses set farther apart. She stopped for a minute, turned around in a circle, but still couldn't place where she was. She kept walking then made a left turn, hoping this would take her back to her original spot. Further up, she saw a few people coming out of a store. Well, she thought, at least I can get the milk.

As she walked in, Safia noticed that the young man at the cash register had black hair, heavy eyebrows, and dark eyes set deep in his face. Not Egyptian, she thought, but could be something else, maybe Lebanese. She walked down the narrow aisles. It was a small convenience food store with lots of canned goods and a refrigerator full of beer. She sighted the milk and made her way toward it. But, as she entered the last aisle, her steps halted. Her nose twitched with a familiar smell although she couldn't name it. She looked and to her left there were a line of covered bins. She opened the first one, and it was *borghul,* the brown wheat she mixed with ground meat to make *kobeba.* The next bin had dried fava beans and the next *smeet,* the fine flour she used to make the sweet *basboosa.* She looked up and on the shelf there was the rose water for the baklava.

There were some smaller bins, and there she found cumin, not like in the supermarket where it was held tight in a jar that had probably been sitting on the shelf for years, but fresh, its aroma rising and spreading to the other foods. The smell that her nose had initially caught came from the next bin. She dipped her finger into it, so that the spice formed a small circle on her fingertip. She tasted it; this was the *boharat* she needed. Toward the end of the aisle, she opened another bin, and there were the orange lentils. She dipped her hand inside and scooped them up. As she lifted her hand, some of the orange circles sifted through her fingers. The rest settled into a small mound in her palm.

Airport

He paced the airport waiting room, his steps marking a path in the carpet between the rows of seats. At first, those sitting down looked up at this man who could not hold his feet still like the rest of them and curb his agitation. After a while, some returned to their own thoughts or families. A few kept their gaze on his coming and going, perhaps to ease their own turmoil. Even after he left, a few repeated his path with their eyes as if permanently held by the ghost of his movement.

Samir was about five-foot-seven, with black hair cut short because otherwise it would frizz and wave. His nose was rather large, but his eyes compensated, their brown glimmer and long lashes giving his face an unexpected beauty. He was slender, his physique almost that of a young boy. But around the middle a slight roundness was beginning, probably because for the past year he had been going to a Chinese restaurant and ordering pupu platters for dinner. Once, his coworkers had talked him into going out after work. He was frightened at the prospect of having to understand the menu and perhaps not having enough money. When they ordered something to be shared, he was relieved. The assortment of fried foods soothed him. Although some of the tastes were unfamiliar, he had grown up with the smell of food frying. His mother fried fish, potatoes, cauliflower, so now he could eat with a certain security. He asked a couple of times what this was called, his tongue moving silently in his mouth to repeat the words "pupu platter." After that, occasionally, he would go to the restaurant alone and order the same thing. He didn't catch the odd twist of the waiter's face, and he ate confidently.

It was eleven o'clock Sunday morning. He had woken early, a little before six, despite having stayed up late cleaning his small apartment thoroughly. Glancing at his watch, he noted there was still another hour before the plane was due. He extended his pacing out of the waiting area to look at one of the screens showing arrivals and departures. Flight 822 from Egypt via Switzerland. Yes, the arrival time was still twelve p.m. He turned his gaze around the airport until his eyes fell on some tables and chairs that he hoped were part of a coffee shop. He headed over, lengthening his stride a little. Ordering the coffee, he was tempted to get something to eat but was afraid his stomach would turn, so he settled at a small table with the styrofoam cup awkwardly balanced in his hand. It was too hot to drink, so he could only sit, the sounds of the airport mingling together till they became a steady hum in his head.

She stared at the empty suitcase on her bed. How do you pack for moving to another country? she thought. She circled the room, stopping to sift through open dresser drawers, to flip through clothes hung in the closet, to slightly rearrange items on top of dressers, only to find herself back in front of an empty suitcase.

Her mother appeared at the door. "Hoda, you haven't done anything! The suitcase is empty."

Hoda shifted her eyes to the suitcase as if seeing its open cavity for the first time. "I will. I'm just organizing," Hoda replied to appease her mother.

"You leave early in the morning," her mother said as if ringing a bell.

As her mother stepped out of the room, Hoda sat on the bed, turning her back to the suitcase. She was an attractive woman, but not in the traditional Egyptian sense. Her body was slim without the usual roundness around the hips and legs, probably because she insisted on walking everywhere. Taxis are too expensive and buses are too crowded, she argued. Her black hair was cut straight just above her shoulders. She never put anything in it, didn't use henna, and wore it simply as it was. Her mother had tried to coax her a little, to style it in some way, but after all these years, she knew it was a useless effort. Hoda's face held the energy of youth, and people often found themselves looking at her. It was her mouth that was her most prominent feature. Although it was considered slightly large, there was still something captivating about it, the way her smile pulled you in and made you listen to whatever she was saying,

It was eleven o'clock Saturday morning. She had woken early, a little before six, despite having stayed up late saying good-bye to friends and relatives. The first thing she did was call the airport to check the departure time. Flight 822 to Boston via Switzerland. Yes, it was leaving at two in the morning and due to arrive at 12 p.m. American Eastern time. After she hung up, she made herself a cup of coffee, although she rarely drank it. The traffic outside began its erratic rhythm of fitful stops and starts accentuated by the loud honks of impatient drivers. She sat in the kitchen almost in a trance until her ears tuned the noise outside to a steady hum in her head.

Would she be on the plane? It was his brother who had written with the flight information. He had received one letter from her parents, accepting his proposal and giving their blessing. Everything else, signing the church marriage papers, processing the immigration documents, had been done through his brother. And it had taken longer than expected, almost two years of filling out forms, presenting proof of this and that, till he felt his life had transformed into a sheaf of papers. He sometimes forgot the purpose behind all this, that it would eventually lead to marrying someone whom he didn't know. At times, fear chimed through Samir's body. Perhaps he should've listened when his brother had urged him to return to Egypt, to choose for himself. But Samir was reluctant to leave his new job.

In the meantime, all he could do was wait and work. He had arrived in this country with little money and little education. The only school that would accept him in Egypt was the agricultural college. For two years, he sat and listened to professors lecturing about crops, soil, irrigation till his mind blurred and he knew if he didn't leave, he would end up another man with a college degree selling cigarettes in a kiosk. He was not a lucky person, but he entered the immigration lottery anyway. It was free, and they only asked for your name and address. The rumor said fifty thousand each year would be chosen to come to America. And he had heard of people who won and actually went. What a strange country, he thought, to make its immigration decisions through a lottery. He curbed his joy when he received notification that he had been selected. It was clear that the process would be long. Now came the applications to be filled, the requests for documents, the interview questions answered in halting English, which he felt sure would eliminate him, but the end was indeed permission to emigrate, to chance his life in another country.

≈

Would he be there? What was she doing going to another country to marry a man she didn't even know? Her parents had helped convince her that this would be best for her. "He's from a good family, and after all, he's in America and not many people can get there." "Besides," her father added, "this America is more suited to your independent nature." "Yes," her mother added in a resigned tone, "and they like educated people there." It was true that in Egypt Hoda often felt like a piece of rough wood that needed to be sanded down. No one understood her desire to continue for a master's degree in chemistry. "You have a college degree," her parents argued, "and you're twenty-one now. Look for a husband. It's time to settle down." When a young man approached her parents to propose marriage, she had accepted, thinking this would keep people quiet. But she had been naive. The young man was insistent that she quit school and devote her time to setting up their new home. Finally their heated arguments led to breaking the engagement, and not surprisingly, this only worsened her reputation. She knew her parents feared that now she would never marry.

When the proposal from America came, she hesitated. She had one more year until she completed her degree. But everyone assured her the paperwork would allow her enough time to finish. And they were right. Things dragged out for so long that at times she forgot she was engaged or that she was going to America. So when Samir's brother appeared at their door two weeks ago with the plane tickets and the approved visa, her head spun like a top.

Samir had arrived in America with some hope and trepidation. The process had been difficult, but each time he pictured himself standing inside a kiosk, his body trapped and his arms reaching for cigarettes, he was able to push himself and do what was requested. Surely in America there would be more possibilities. But that first year, America kept him dog-paddling and gasping for air. The language confounded him, quick mutterings with hardly any gestures or even a direct look. He took an English class, but the rules of grammar and the purposely slow pronunciation of the teacher did little to improve his understanding. He found a job washing dishes in a restaurant where contact was limited to "Good morning," "How are you," and "See you later." When the radio in the kitchen broke one day, followed by the mumbled swearing of the cook, he offered to fix it. The cook gave him a perplexed look and tossed the radio to him with a "Go ahead." The dishes piled up a bit as he fiddled with the switches, found a knife to use as a screwdriver, and then managed to make the music reemerge. After that, other radios and sometimes clocks, telephones, or calculators were handed to him. Most of the time he could fix them, and the added conversations made him more confident.

Fixing things was the one thing he could do. It was like a sixth sense to him. When he was a child, if something broke at home, they couldn't afford to buy another one. Since it was already not working, his family figured there was no harm in letting him fiddle with it, and so he learned how everything was put together, how to take it apart, and how to reconnect the parts so it worked. He was most comfortable staring at the inside of a machine with its intricate weaving of wires and knobs. But he had never perceived his ability as a skill; it was simply an instinct.

When the restaurant manager caught wind of his reputation, he approached him with a request to fix his stereo, adding, "I took it to the shop but they couldn't do anything."

He spent a day at the manager's house, surrounded by components with wires stretching like a web of animal tails. Every time the manager walked by, Samir saw him shaking his head with a look of doubt clouding his face. By the end of the day, the tails had been untangled, and when Samir pressed the power button, the music spread through the house. "Thank you, thank you," the manager repeated, and Samir stood, puzzled by how a boss could lower himself to thank an employee. The manager sent Samir to the same shop that couldn't fix his stereo. He was hired on a trial basis, but he proved himself quickly. He had found his niche in this country that could make many things, but didn't know how to fix what it broke.

It wasn't that Hoda didn't want to get married. She had always hoped her life would be with a partner, and at some point she expected to have children. But she knew she didn't want the life she saw around her. Women dragging their chores like chains, cleaning house, washing clothes, cooking food, all for others. She had watched friends marry at eighteen and nineteen, sometimes even men of their own choosing whom they loved. Within the first year, their spirits dissipated like sugar crystals in water. It frightened her to envision her life in this way, her days filled with the care of home and family, her body growing heavy with the idleness of her brain.

That is why, against everyone's understanding, she enrolled in the master's program in chemistry. She was one of two women, but the other was there only to pass the time until she found a husband. Her family had determined that it would be more respectable for her to continue her studies than to remain at home waiting. But for Hoda, it was a different matter. Chemistry had caught her fancy, and it was the only thing she wanted to do. As a child her mother had to pull her out of the kitchen, where she would find her sitting cross-legged on the floor with a bowl in front of her, mixing starch and water, baking soda and vinegar, or some new combination. "Just to see what would happen," she answered her mother's shouting inquiries. Finally, her mother banished her from the kitchen. The result, aside from Hoda never learning how to cook, was that she began borrowing chemistry books from her friend's older brother who was studying at the university and moved the experiments to more secluded parts of the house. She struggled through the master's program, where the male students laughed directly at her, and the professors didn't take her seriously. Still she persisted and gained high marks. It was an act of faith since she knew the only job Egypt would give her would be in a lab analyzing blood and urine samples.

Perhaps that's why she accepted the roll of dice that would

lead her to America. There might be a chance there of having a real job, of doing research, of working with someone who would respect her, not turn everything back around to her femininity. Her English was strong since all the sciences were taught in English, and she had occasionally had American or British professors with whom she had no trouble communicating. What concerned her was this man who had extended his proposal across the ocean. What kind of man would marry a woman without even seeing her, would choose as if picking a number out of a hat?

≈

After two years in America and turning thirty, Samir knew he had to get married. He also knew he needed a certain kind of woman, not one who would lean on him, who would expect to be at home while he worked. He needed someone who could stand in this world next to him, perhaps even lead him a little. He sent his request to his brother: a woman who was educated, who knew English well, who wanted to work; a woman who could swim in deep water, he added. His brother argued that he was asking for trouble, that such women should remain unmarried. But Samir was insistent and said he would accept nothing else.

≈

Hoda was twenty-five years old. If she didn't marry soon, she would be looked on with either pity or suspicion. And if she remained in Egypt and married the next man who proposed, her life would inevitably fall into the repeated pattern of other women. She couldn't articulate what she wanted, only that it was not here.

Hoda caught her breath like the reins of a horse and began

to fill the suitcases. She counted the number of dresses, skirts, and pants she had, then divided by half: that's how many she would take. Then she proceeded to do the same with all other items. Within a few hours, the two permitted suitcases were filled.

DREAMS OF RETURN

Phone Call Three

Aloo—*Aloo*—yes—who is calling—*Aloo*—mama—what is wrong—yes, we're well—are you well—is something wrong mama—yes, yes, we are all well—mama is there something wrong—uncle uncle is he well—what—*baba*—no—how—his heart—as soon as he woke up—it can't be true—no—how mama—tomorrow is the funeral—right away—no—it's impossible—we'll come as soon as we can—soon mama—*ensha allah* god willing—yes, it's two in the morning—six hours difference—no, it doesn't matter—it's good that you called me right away—it's eight o'clock in the morning there—ok—*ensha allah* god willing we will come soon—*ma elsalama ya mama*

A Conversation

> "You want me to go back? I'm sixty-five years old."

My hair is gray, and my body has grown into its age. I have settled into myself. No longer the young girl you met, the one who flirted and teased, who wore her black hair like a shield, enticing you to ask for her hand. No longer the one who agreed to wrap herself around you and fly across the ocean, willing to release each strand that held me close to family and home, believing in this miracle of America. I'm old, and my steps are solid on this land where I have learned to live; they cannot turn around now and go in a different direction.

> "We can retire there. Do you know how much our money is worth? I can buy a beautiful apartment. We can live on the *corniche* and look at the Nile every day."

I left, only a young man with little in my pocket. My family held me back, ridiculed my dreams, told me I would never make it in America, that my life could only be wrapped in this place with a job pushing me each day to make only enough to feed us and hold a roof over our heads, that I was a fool to imagine myself in the open space of a new land, that I would return to beg for a morsel of food. Now my money can take me back to every ice cream my mouth drooled for as a young child. These dollars I have bought and sold will multiply till they're an endless chain of pearls. Like the rich, we can buy an apartment, two stories, with marble floors and gold faucets, and a balcony that lifts us above the city so our eyes can stretch over the Nile each day.

> **"We've been in this country for forty years."**

Forty years is a lifetime. Your mother died before she turned fifty; her heart failed after we left. You could not even tell her the truth about our immigration, trying to convince her it was only a short excursion, a youthful desire to see the magic of the other side of the world. But she looked at our faces, the anxiety of our anticipation, and she knew that her only son was leaving. My father died only years later, barely reaching the age of sixty. We could not even return so I could stand by mother's side as she buried him. Forty years we have built a life and left one behind.

> **"You can have everything there. I'll buy you whatever you want."**

Those early years, every penny we had to hold tight in our fists. I watched you cut coupons, squint your eyes at the price tags, and stretch each pound of meat with bread. Every birthday I failed you, and even a single rose was an extravagance I held back. There I can buy you dresses to sparkle on your body, jewels to circle your wrists; whatever your eye rests on, I'll offer you as my gift. Don't you want to enter a store and lay your finger on any item, to have it be yours like the magic of wishes coming true?

> **"And do you have enough money to get rid of the pollution and the crowds too?"**

When we decided to go and everyone's talk of foolish dreams and the struggle of America failed to keep our feet still, my father sold his land by the pyramids so we could have something to hold us as we began our new lives. My mother took off her gold bracelet with its snakes intertwining around her wrist and sold it so there was enough to buy the tickets. What can your money buy for us now? The streets in Cairo are brimming with the poor and hopeful, and their dreams release the stench caught in our nostrils. You can't walk without the weight of people bumping against you and inhaling the fumes of smoke and garbage. Our money will not release us from the city's grabbing fist.

> **"We can go to the Red Sea. We'll buy a chalet, and we can go when we like."**

Do you remember our honeymoon in Hurghada? We rented a small chalet, and each morning the slender waves lapped at our door. I held your hand as we crossed the sand, and we walked toward the corals beneath the surface, laughing when the tiny fish nibbled at our ankles. I unfolded my arms like a hammock to hold your body so the sea could carry you. And at night, the sand winds whistled at our door as we floated inside each other, my body surprised by the softness of your skin like the caress of each wave. The beach was almost empty that October, and we owned each grain of sand as we spoke our dreams like the drops of water glistening on our skin. We'll buy a chalet to make it our own, a place we can inhabit at our will. We'll own the corals and the waves and the sun's dreams, walk across the edge of sand, marking our ground.

> **"After we've come here and struggled and built a life?"**

You couldn't find a job, and when you came home, I saw your face like a stone engraved in silence. You took a job washing dishes. Your hands became red and brittle, the fingers bending in and your knuckles hardening against the harsh soap. A year until finally you found something in a small company, each day sitting at your desk. But I knew the boss looked over your shoulder, touching his pen to your work, marking corrections. You stooped over that desk for years, the fear of losing the job etched in your eyes. I found work, punching in time cards, leaving my children in day-care centers, afraid I would forget their faces. It took years till we saved enough that you could shrug off the choke of having a boss and strike out on your own. We have built this life with our hands; each stone in this house we have carried on our backs.

"We can live like royalty there."

What do we have here? Our house we pay for each month, the bank looming over us. It is empty space, the walls turning their corners, tucking us inside their angles, keeping us cloistered. We live like monks, our lives restricted. In Egypt, our hands would touch nothing. We can purchase each task: a servant to clean the house, a man to deliver the groceries, a cook to stand in the kitchen. And we would be free to come and go as we please. We can stay at the Oberoi Hotel in Giza, lounge at the pool, and watch the sun set over the pyramids, each drink and each plate delivered to us. Imagine your life at your fingertips, only making the request to have it be granted.

"These are dreams. No one lives like a king there."

You remember only the beauty of things; maybe that is why I married you. Your eyes have always stretched their vision beyond the boundaries of the horizon; you follow a dream that no one else can see. Egypt has no more kings or queens. Its days of glory are over. The country is crowded only with leftover peasants. The kings gathered their wealth and ran, leaving only those who know how to struggle for the same bread they eat daily. Their bare feet are caked with the mud of the Nile as they carry their loads and scrape their few piasters each day. The river's water has become poisonous, and the land abandoned to those who cannot nurture it.

> **"Over there life is good, and the people have morals."**

A sense of decency. People look in your face. Greet you with respect. We take care of each other—not like here, abandoned, every man for himself and no one stops to help lift those who fall. People can still feel with their hearts. There, even those who have nothing share their bite of food.

> **"Over there people are eating each other and everyone is just for himself. You've forgotten why we came."**

The corruption. The bribes. The connections you need to take even a small step. The poor scramble for a few scraps of nourishment, while the rich play their monopoly with real money. There is nothing but the hardship of each day. Each man tumbling over the next to win.

> **"We'll have everything. At least people will respect us. Not like here. Forty years and the Americans still look at us as if we were cockroaches walking on their land."**

I have learned their language, their slang, their clothing, how to eat their food, how to laugh at their jokes, how to make their money. Still they grimace when they meet me, they scratch their heads instead of shaking my hand, they scowl when they learn I live in the best neighborhood. I changed my name, so I could erase the sour look on their face when I introduce myself. America welcomes you into its land so you can mop its floors. I want to hold my head up high again, to breathe my name and have it heard.

> **"What are you saying? We found good work, and we bought a house. Our children got educated here. You want me to go back and not see them?"**

Look, look, at what we have. This house that is large and grand. In Egypt, we would have stayed in that two-bedroom apartment. I found a job here and went in each day to earn our living. No one harassed me, and no one told me I wasn't smart enough. We raised our sons in this house instead of cramming them between the walls and the alleys. We paid for their education with our blood, and one is a doctor and one is an engineer. In that country, they would have stepped on them like vermin because they're Christian; every door shut in their faces till we would have been lucky to see them sweep the streets for a living.

> **"They'll come visit us."**

We'll bring them to see us. They will know where they are from, and they will be part of their family. They will bring their children to play on the sand and bounce in the waves of the sea like you and I did when we were young. We will pull our family together again and loosen the tight grip of isolation. We will all return to settle our feet into the sand and water of our homeland.

> **"You're dreaming. Our children will never leave this country."**

Your thoughts are like a fairy tale; you weave light and air to make a tapestry of magic colors. Our sons have settled their lives in this country. They have found a place for themselves, and already they are piling the stones to build a home for their children. From their birth, they claimed this land as their own, and the thread that ties them to Egypt has become a thin sliver too invisible to follow back.

> **"I want to live the rest of my life in peace without struggling."**

To look out on the sea and own the world.

> **"I came here, and I'm going to die here."**

This life I have built, I will not let it go.

The Dancer

The belly dancer rotated her hips, a taut wire directing the fluid movement of her bare midriff. Her smile tugged at the corners of her lips to sustain the hint of sincerity. The music from the small band, a keyboard, oud, and tabla, blared through the oversized speakers in the church hall. Long tables crowded against the walls, allowing a small dance area to open in the middle of the floor. Bright neon lights glared over the hall, casting everyone equally and keeping the shadows tucked in corners. The dancer switched her movements to a quicker step, revolving her body to circle the floor while facing the tables. Her pale blue outfit jingled with the gold and silver disks attached to the skirt and top. She kept one leg pushed out of the side slit of the skirt, revealing the practiced muscles of her body.

The wedding had started at 8:00 p.m. After the long ceremony crowning the bride and groom to join them for life, there was the line of guests giving their congratulations and kisses to the new couple till their cheeks felt indented with the force of good wishes. Finally, the reception had started with the bride and groom being ushered in by the customary belly dancer. They were met with ululations and joyful shouts as they entered the hall. Now the young couple sat at the head table. The groom's eyes strayed after the belly dancer's swift steps, watching her body curve in and out of the music. The bride's gaze was distracted by friends and family who came to whisper over the loud music, wishing her happiness and giving her small bits of advice.

Sitting at the end of one of the tables in the middle of the hall, Sherif had turned his chair to face the dance floor, and as the dancer approached, he opened his arms, snapping his fingers to the music. She widened her smile and paused her body in front of him to display the controlled shaking of her breasts. Sherif let out a laugh and encouraged her on. The beat of the tabla heightened as she danced. Then she bent to drop a kiss on his cheek and moved to the next table. The guests at his table let out a score of jokes and innuendos, while Sherif responded in like manner. Only his wife, Mounira, who sat at the other end of the table nearest the wall, was quiet, her lips drawing a thin, slivered line across her face.

The belly dancer continued her flirtation around the dance floor, and each time she paused in front of Sherif as he drew her toward him with his laughter and gestures. Sherif's hazel eyes followed each calculated motion of her body, responding to the music of her movement. Now nearing sixty, Sherif was no longer the attractive man he had been in his youth. His hair, predominantly white and thin, had pulled back from his forehead, giving his face an egg-like appearance. His love of sweets resulted in a rounded belly, making his hips look narrower. But people still turned to look, catching the sparkle in his eyes that made them want to join in his pleasure. He was at his best amidst a crowd, creating a fervor of excitement that made others feel they were at the center of some significant event. And, like today, he could always draw a performer toward him; despite his aging appearance, they gravitated like butterflies to nectar.

The band and dancer took a break so dinner could be served. Sherif received a few slaps on the back as he made his way through the buffet line. Mounira stayed at the table a little longer, waiting till the line had filtered through. She avoided glancing toward Sherif. "He can make a fool of himself," she thought, "but I'll have no part in it." She let her body settle more solidly into her chair, so the straight lines of the table pressed against her own rounded shape. As a young woman, Mounira had held some attractiveness. Her small-boned stature gave her an aura of delicacy that suggested gracefulness. She was slender enough that her shoulder blades protruded slightly, giving her body the feel of a textured surface. Although her hips rounded out and her thighs lay thick, people rarely noticed, describing her instead as petite and thin.

The buffet line shortened, and someone tapped Mounira to get up and join. She half smiled and pushed back her chair, awkwardly scraping the floor. The chair didn't move enough, and she had to squeeze herself out. She walked steadily to the buffet table. Over the years, her body had filled itself out so that now the upper and lower half had achieved an awkward balance. Her face still held its oval shape, but the rest of her had expanded so she resembled those Russian dolls that contained a series of smaller dolls inside. Perhaps the last doll would be her first body still slender and youthful.

Mounira saw Sherif as she made her way back to the table. He was eating with gusto, the shish kebab, rice, and eggplant piled on his plate. He did not look at her, and she returned to her seat.

"Your husband is quite the partier," the woman across the table said.

"Yes," replied Mounira, smiling a little too wide and revealing the gap in her teeth.

She bit into another piece of lamb quickly and started chewing. She had always been conscious of the gap in her mouth. People thought she had a tooth pulled, but in truth, when she had lost her baby tooth, a new one never came in to take its place. She had waited and waited, but the gap remained. Sometimes she still flicked the opening with her tongue, imagining she could feel the rough edge of a new tooth.

When the music started again, the belly dancer came out, this time to gather her payment as both children and adults took turns tucking bills into her costume. Sherif got up and danced with her for a minute before tucking a twenty-dollar bill at each of her breasts. Mounira turned to her cup of coffee, tasting its last grainy sip.

"Lighten up," her cousin said, poking her in the ribs. "He's just having fun."

Mounira stretched her lips into a thin line, creating something that might be mistaken for a smile. She was grateful that her cousin had turned her gaze toward the dance floor again.

The rest of the evening was spent eating, drinking, and congratulating the bride and groom. A few of the teenagers got up and danced to the band's attempt at Western music. Sherif continued to drink and joke, occasionally enticing one of the young girls to dance with him. Despite his age, his body could still sway to the beat of the music, mimicking the energy of a more youthful man. He walked over to Mounira, urging her to a slow dance. But she shook her head without looking at him.

"I have a headache," she said.

And he went off with a shrug to get another drink.

The guests began to leave around one in the morning. Sherif and Mounira got in their car, a black Cadillac that Sherif had insisted on buying two years ago. Mounira shifted her weight to the middle of the seat while Sherif waved goodbye to other guests and slipped into the driver's side. Mounira curved into herself. She would say nothing, she decided. She would not give him the satisfaction of her anger. Sherif began to drive and the car filled with their silence.

"It was a nice party," Sherif ventured, speaking toward the windshield.

Mounira took in a shallow breath in response.

They drove through the darkened streets of the city, an occasional glimmer of light rising from the water's surface when they passed the river.

"The food was good," added Sherif.

"Yes, so was the belly dancer," Mounira said, the words slipping air between her teeth.

"Are you angry again?" asked Sherif, his back straightening against the seat.

"Why should I be angry?" The words tumbled out of Mounira's mouth more rapidly than she had intended.

Mounira tried to take a deeper breath without making any noticeable noise. "I will not get angry," she repeated to herself. She shifted her weight only to end up in the same position. "It doesn't matter what he does," she continued the argument in her head. "It has nothing to do with me. I don't care."

"I was just having a good time, like everybody else," Sherif explained, rolling the window down a few inches then closing it again.

"The belly dancer didn't kiss anyone else. She didn't shake her breasts in front of anyone else's face." Mounira caught her breath before more words escaped.

"She just liked me," Sherif said with a slight smirk forming in the corner of his mouth.

There were no other cars and the road held them in its grasp as they drove.

"At least I didn't sit still in the same chair all night like some statue," Sherif retorted, although she had said nothing.

"You needn't worry about me. I had a perfectly good time, and I didn't make a fool of myself." Mounira folded her arms across her chest although the posture made her uncomfortable.

"You think anyone who is having a little fun is making a fool of themselves. It was all in good spirit," Sherif answered in explanation.

Mounira unfolded her arms, letting her chest expand. "Maybe for you it's fun. I think it's cheap and insulting. What are people going to think? How do you think it makes me feel? Sitting there watching you. Like I'm not even there. It's disrespectful. It's just disgusting."

Sherif turned the car into the driveway of their suburban home, allowing the argument to stall.

They went into the house and got ready for bed, keeping the stony silence between them.

Mounira had slipped on her nightgown before Sherif locked the doors and came upstairs. She went into the bathroom to take off her makeup and brush her hair. This was not how she had imagined her life. The curtain of tension between them, each year adding a layer. The distance opening a gulf that trapped her. She had dreamed that marriage would free her. She would be away from her parents' vigilant eyes and evenings would be filled with social gatherings where she would shine each night, wearing a different dress. She had imagined herself through the years, her body holding its youthful, slender tone, the arch of her shoulders still curved and angular. She had not dreamed the weight of childbirth, the infant mouth on her breast that would suck her dry, or the way her body would push closer to the earth every year, her weight heavier on each foot.

She came out of the bathroom and got into bed where Sherif was already lying down, his eyes closed. She turned the light off and slid her body under the covers. The images of the evening floated in her mind: the beautiful bride, the dancer ushering them in, the dancer hugging Sherif to her chest. Mounira blinked her eyes, willing the images to close. She felt Sherif's hand on her back, moving slightly. She held her breath.

His touch moved down her back to her waist. He slid his arm around her. Sherif felt the warmth of her skin through the nightgown. He knew she wasn't sleeping. Her breath hadn't fallen into its regular pattern. She was so young and beautiful when he married her; she reminded him of the hand blown glass he had seen being made one day at the Pharaonic Village on a school trip. He watched as the man blew, filling the air with a liquid that slowly hardened into a solid shape. He had been afraid to come near her, fearing his touch would break her. Her skin was light and smooth. She seemed almost transparent when he touched her. Now she lay next to him, more solid than he could have imagined. But he wanted to reach her, to find the core he had longed for when he married her. After all these years, he still sometimes felt as if he had never made love to her.

Sherif's hand slid under her nightgown to her breasts. Mounira said nothing but allowed her body to unfold slightly. She felt him tugging at her nightgown and helped him to lift it over her head. The covers slid to her waist, and she pulled them back up. Sherif kissed her. His lips were wet and hard against her mouth. She tried not to turn away.

Sherif wanted to say something, to ask if it was all right, if she wanted to, but the words remained unspoken. He lifted himself above her, urging her legs open. Slowly, he let his body slide over her so he could feel her move against him. He found his way inside her, but she lay beneath him, an intangible thing.

Aisle Three

She could hold her breath, balance the tightrope traffic of carts until the third aisle of the supermarket. Then, usually by the pasta, her eyes would dart to a stop, and she would be still, looking, looking through shells, twirls, and bows till her gaze bounced back to move her again. Sometimes, if she kept her footing steady, if she had a list, if she crossed out each item diligently, if she didn't lose her pen by the green onions, she could continue all the way to the frozen-food aisles where the chill air would hold her frame against the door. Someone would open it, and as it snapped back airtight, the frost would gather to eliminate her shadow.

Once it happened in the produce section. The mangoes stopped her, scattered in an end aisle bin, their green skin tight-wrapped and firm. Surprised to find them, she cradled her long fingers around one, lifted it to her nose. Inhaling only the over-ripe odor of nearby dented tomatoes, she sniffed harder, drawing in until some slight sweetness entered her nostrils. In childhood, the mango was cut in half against its oval seed then sliced into squares and the skin bent back to prop up each bite, sweet juice dripping down her chin. In August when the fruit's season swept through the heavy heat of the city, the mangos would appear piled like step pyramids against each storefront. Soraya looked down and turned the mango over face up in her palm to see a patch of slight red marking the one ripe spot.

The mangos were $2.99 each, so she placed the one in her hand back among the rest and pushed her cart ahead.

It had been difficult coming to this supermarket for the past five years now, with its waxed cucumbers, wrinkled zucchini, and baggers who commented on the large quantity of her purchases. There was no sense explaining that she tried to shop only once a month in order to avoid the chore or that she had two adolescent boys whose appetites consumed her purchases like a gulp of water. There were somewhat better supermarkets, and sometimes she called up enough energy to drive the extra distance to them. But more often she settled for the convenience of this one, claiming the short distance allowed her time to do her other household tasks.

She wondered if her laziness was due to age. Soraya felt strange thinking of herself as forty-two. She still felt ill at ease in her adulthood. But when she caught a glimpse of herself, she saw it was true. Her body seemed to have settled into itself, a little heavier now and more solid. It made her feel attached to the ground, and even her dreams of flying had stopped. Her brown complexion had acquired a different shade in the hot southern sun, and sometimes her darkness surprised her in the mirror. She cut her black hair to her shoulders, as once she heard her aunt say an older woman shouldn't have long hair. Surprisingly, there were few white hairs and it was still thick. The slight hint of green in her eyes rarely appeared now, and it seemed as if their brown was darkening.

Moving to this small town in Virginia was not what Soraya had expected after years of watching her husband earn his PhD. Somehow she had assumed they would stay in New England, maybe even in Boston, the city she had learned to wrap around herself like a night cloak. The pattern of her days filled with subways, walks to the Middle Eastern grocery store, and sometimes a stop for a cappuccino, the foam reminding her of cream scooped off boiling milk and mixed with sugar to put on jam for breakfast. The routine was consistent enough to keep her balanced. And the secretarial job in the art department suited her once she adjusted to the students' blue hair and eyebrow piercings. She kept her attention on their registration forms and updating the frequently changing faculty schedules. She hadn't realized how familiar her life had become until it was time to move.

It began with the mad rush of typing her husband's dissertation, formatting, acid-free paper, his defense, and ended with the one job offer from a small college in Virginia.

She packed, arranged for moving companies, found an apartment, enrolled her children in the local school. But it was as if one part of her was closing without another opening. Now, after six years, one son was twelve and the other fourteen. Yet, she felt as if at any moment, she would walk back through a door and find them still her young children, not these adolescents for whom she could do nothing but feed and wash clothes.

Soraya stopped at the canned beans. Chickpeas, she thought, I can make hummus. She had bought them here a few times. Not seeing them right away, she knelt and began looking behind the cans of black-eyed peas and kidney beans. Nothing. "Where are they," she asked, "I found them here before." She put the cans on the floor to reach further back. "They must have some. No one else buys them."

"Excuse me," she heard someone say.

Holding her tongue, she mumbled in Arabic *you donkey* and shifted her weight so the customer could get by. Finally, she got up. "Chickpeas, you'd think they'd have chickpeas," she said as her eyes kept traveling the shelves, "They're not exotic; they're just chickpeas." A customer turned to look at her.

Soraya snapped her hands onto the cart and turned the corner out of the aisle.

She was seventeen when her parents decided to emigrate, leaving a comfortable life in Cairo. But it was worth it, everyone said, for her older brother, Walid, to go to medical school in America. Soraya was perplexed by the move. No one asked her what she wanted to do; she was like another bag to be packed, making sure it didn't exceed the weight allowance. She had never felt the pressure that other girls without brothers sometimes felt, to become a doctor or engineer, to bring honor to the family. That was her brother's role.

Soraya simply walked alongside her family through the airport metal detectors.

Each year in Virginia, she had uttered her disappointment. Her husband agreed and applied for a few jobs. Nothing was offered, and they said next year maybe, and stayed. She adjusted somewhat, enough to live a daily life. It took a while to become accustomed to the constant smiles and waving. People waved as she drove by, and when she tried to wave back, she would almost swerve off the road, unable to steer with one hand while looking to identify the other person. Finally, toward the end of the first year, she figured out that if she kept her thumb hooked onto the steering wheel and waved with only four fingers, she could keep the car straight. It was a small success. But she couldn't break through the isolation. It encircled her, and tapping for an opening yielded nothing. She thought about working again, but each year they expected to leave so the effort to find a job eluded her. She consumed her time with the housework, cooking, and shopping, all the necessary tasks.

The mountains surrounded her, and she heard people exclaim at their beauty. One winter, she overheard someone remark, "They're beautiful this time of year; they look almost pink." So she looked and yes, they were pink. But she couldn't find the beauty in them. Bald and pink, she thought. They stood still except when they closed in on her, their movements like stealth. Maybe it was too much nature, she guessed. Boston was the only place in this country where she had felt some ease. It must have been all that concrete, reminiscent of Cairo with its spindly trees propped out of sidewalks and no flowers except those sold on street corners. Each year, she encouraged her husband to apply to jobs in New York, Philadelphia, Detroit, Chicago; all she needed, she thought, was concrete and crowds. Here, there was too much green and no other Arabs or immigrants that she could find, unlike Boston, where she saw herself reflected in variations.

Today she had left her husband at home alone, so he could work on his tenure portfolio due at the end of the month. He assured her it didn't mean he would stop applying, but he had to submit the portfolio; it was necessary. She knew he would receive tenure. He had done his job well, and everyone liked him with his easy smile and ability to make his students feel important. She too had been attracted by that smile, but mostly it was his sense of certainty, as if he held a deed to each place he walked. Born and raised in the Midwest, her husband's sense of belonging had helped keep her precarious hold steady all these years. There were times when she would have liked him to understand Arabic so she wouldn't have to search so hard for the English word or to wake up one morning and ask her to make fava beans for breakfast. But she held those desires in check like her craving for pickled lemons.

She knew he would get tenure and they would stay and this would be her future.

Soraya looked at her cart. She was halfway through the supermarket and had put nothing in it. Perhaps she should go back to Egypt for a visit. The thought of another long flight made her shudder. She felt a slight push at her back and heard someone say "I'm sorry" and pull their cart away. She was in the crackers and chips aisle. Nothing here, she thought and continued.

Bread, she would buy bread. "Even here they have Syrian bread," she mumbled to herself. "Not very good, but it will do." Her eyes traveled up and down the shelves. In college, her roommate had once complained that every time she asked Soraya to buy bread, she wouldn't buy the normal kind. Soraya's eyebrows had wrinkled in confusion. "I mean," her roommate explained, "that you always buy *pita* bread, not normal bread." Soraya finally found it, but it was a different brand. She reached for a package and stared at it. The round thin loaves were smaller and thicker than they should be. Soraya let her body sink to the floor so she could look more closely. "It's perforated," she said loudly, "the bread is perforated. What? You need directions to eat Syrian bread? Don't people know what to do with a piece of bread, this bread you tear with your hands to dip into tahini, to scoop up beans." Her words drifted between Arabic and English as she opened the package to stare at the dashes, machine made in a precise line across each loaf.

"Excuse me, Ma'am, you can't open the food in the store. Excuse me, Ma'am, but you have to get up."

Soraya heard nothing as she took each loaf out of the bag and tore it into pieces, everywhere except on the line, one after the other.

Oregano

Someone knocked on the door. It startled me as it always does now. I've grown used to being alone, and I have to shake myself to return to the company of others. Days go by and I don't need to say anything to anyone. Even in the grocery store, people look straight ahead, driving their shopping carts like their cars. And the cashier says "How are you ma'am?" to the air above her head; no need to answer. Now they have those fancy new check-yourself-out aisles, so there isn't even a chance to get one of the nice cashiers who might make a little conversation or a bagger to take your cart out for you, say a few words along the way.

So when one of the neighbors drops by like today, my balance is thrown off, and I feel like those pink birds people put in their yard always standing on one leg, except I'm about to tip over. It takes a minute to focus on their face while they talk; I'm used to seeing just the furniture and the pictures on the wall. Well, today it was Diane come chattering at the door carrying one of her stews. Something about a new recipe and hopes that I like it. It's nice of her, bringing food over, except it's always a little spicy, just an odd flavor, something my mouth hasn't had before, and I'm too old for these new tastes to have time to become familiar. Diane's got an herb garden, so she fiddles and tries something new each year. I keep telling her to plant some oregano; good oregano is hard to find, but she's not interested in these old things. I like her though because she walks in the door talking and that gives me time to adjust to someone else being in the house without my ears having to listen too hard. She goes out just as fast, and I don't have a chance to say more than thank you.

I've been in this house alone for almost five years now. My daughters, they keep trying to convince me to sell the house and move into one of those old people commune places. "It'd be better for you Mama," they say. "Someone would take care of all your needs," they argue. I know they just worried about themselves. Where I come from, your children take care of you when you get old just like you take care of them when they're young. It's a circle so it just goes around and things stay the same. There are no nursing homes in Egypt except a few sad ones where those with no family at all end up like torn rags. But I wouldn't want my daughters watching me. They're both out there in California, land of sunshine, they say. But my bones have grown used to the cold. When that chill enters my skin, it just settles in like another layer of insulation.

I came to this country almost fifty years ago even though sometimes it feels like just a few days have passed. My husband and I landed in the middle of winter. We went out to see the world covered with all that snow. Nothing like I had ever known. The only thing we have in Egypt is a few bits of ice that sometimes fall out of the sky. Here, the ground was a solid layer, all white and sparkling. We took a walk in this park, holding on to each other's arms. But we kept slipping, our feet finding nothing to grip. And we laughed out loud as we fell, sliding down on that snow so cold against our thin coats.

It was hard at first, trying to find jobs, a place to live. I'd never worked; all I'd ever done was manage the household budget. My husband, Rafik, he found a job pretty quick because he was an engineer and his English was good. It took me a while. Finally, this Egyptian woman we met told me about filing, how all you had to know was the alphabet. So I memorized those letters, repeating them till they bounced in my head all night. Then I got a job as a filing clerk in a company.

We made a good life here. I was so young when we came, just in my early twenties. My husband wanted to emigrate and so I joined him. Life wasn't easy in Egypt, especially for those of us who are Coptic. Rafik worked so hard, two jobs and sometimes three. Taking trains to Menya and Assiut to teach at the universities there and picking up extra jobs. I didn't see him very often. Still, we were doing well until one of his colleagues got angry because Rafik got promoted before him. He made trouble for him, and it was just too hard. Besides, everyone was talking about leaving so it seemed like the right thing to do.

Both of our daughters were born here. They grew like stalks of wheat soaking in the sun and air of this country. And they're strong now. I don't need to worry about them. But I look at their faces and can't read their eyes. When my first one was born and the nurse handed her to me all pretty wrapped in a pink blanket, I looked at her brown eyes open wide and felt so quick how separate she was from me when just yesterday her body and mine were the same. I knew I couldn't hold her, and everyone thought my eyes tearing because I was so happy.

I just came back from visiting them in California since they kept urging. But that warm air tired out my body, made me feel like I was carrying a load too heavy. They took me to see the sights and wanted me to have a good time. They're both married, working, and living in nice houses. It was good to see them, all grown up and beautiful. But it was hard being around their husbands. They're tall and pale and their faces like a portrait; none of their features move when they talk and their lips so thin, hardly opening to let the words out, so I can't understand what they say. They take up space like a piece of furniture.

Then one day while I'm visiting, they say, "Mama, how about we go look at some nice homes?" At first I thought we were going to look at historic houses again. But when we stopped at the first one, I figured it out pretty quick. These were nursing homes no matter what fancy name they give them. Little apartments, each one like the other. Your eyes grew tired seeing the same shape repeated over and over. How could you tell which one was your own if all the others were all the same? They called those "independent living." Some were just little rooms with one window. "Where all your needs are met," they said. All the while my daughters chattering about how they'd come see me every day, I'd be so close, and it would be such a nice change. I tried to catch some of their enthusiasm. Maybe it would be good to be nearby. It would be nice to see them more often. And some of those apartments weren't so bad, even though the rooms were all the same square shape. And what did I need more than a bedroom and a living room? The kitchens were small, like one of those walk-in closets, everything tightly packed in with just enough space in the middle to stand and turn your face from one appliance to the other. "But you won't need to cook so much," they said, "there's a great cafeteria." "I'll think about it," I promised. And they nodded happily like it was done.

When I got home, there was a note on the door from Diane saying she had a surprise for me and she'd be over later. Probably another fancy dish, I thought. I opened the door and the smell of the house took me in, some combination of furniture polish, the lentil soup I made before leaving, and that musty odor of a house closed up, holding its breath until its owner returns. I carried the suitcase upstairs slowly, my legs aching from sitting on the plane so long. It's hard to do the same things I have always done. My knees hurt when I bend down, and I have to find something to hold on to so I can get up again. And my hands don't always do what I want. The fingers have turned crooked and the knuckles thickened. When I rub them, the skin feels leathery. They're my mother's hands. I know I'm getting old. My body is shorter, heavier, and it creaks like some un-oiled machine. There are only a few strands of black left in my hair; I can almost count them. The skin stretches tighter across my face with lines etched under my eyes and around my chin. Maybe I do need to be in one of those assisted living places. Maybe it is time to let go.

After I unpack, I make myself a cup of mint tea and go out on the back deck. I like to sit out here now. When Rafik was alive, this was his favorite place. I didn't understand why he liked to sit looking at the back of the house. When I had time, I'd go out to the front porch. You could see the other houses, people passing by, and someone might stop to chat. But now I understand how he enjoyed the quiet, being able to look at the world without being pulled into it. And when you sit out here, you can see the whole house from the back. I think he felt sheltered by it.

We bought this house together, almost forty years ago. Every house we saw, there was something we didn't like: too small, too big, street too noisy. When we came to look at this one, I stood in the kitchen feeling the sun come in through all the windows. It was big, with enough room to move around and have a table in the middle for the whole family to eat. I looked out, and there was Rafik standing on the back deck smiling. We caught each other's eye and almost laughed out loud. We each found something we liked and that was our house.

I finish my tea and come back into the kitchen. I should probably go to the supermarket or see what I have to cook, but I just sit down at the table. I look up at the refrigerator. It's covered with pictures from top to bottom. People sent us pictures, and we just put them up there, always managing to find another spot. Our daughters when they were young, wedding pictures, friends, and out of them Rafik's face glimmers. He always smiled in pictures, and sometimes I think if I could just listen hard enough, I'll hear his laugh or see him walking down the stairs.

We were sitting in the living room watching TV. Around

eight o'clock on a Friday. He asked me to get him a glass of water. I went to the kitchen. When I came back to hand it to him, his head was slumped a little to his shoulder and I thought he had fallen asleep. I tapped him on the back but he was gone. Just like that, no warning, nothing to prepare.

Someone must've been knocking for a few minutes because by the time my ears heard, it was a steady, forceful pound. I go over to answer, and there is Diane standing at the door, big smile across her face and a bit of mischief in her eyes. She is carrying a plate of cookies in one hand and a paper bag in the other. She comes in her usual sprightly way, apologizing about how hard she was knocking, how she got worried when I didn't answer, knowing I was supposed to be home by now. She puts the plate on the counter and sits down this time, chatting a bit, asking about my trip. Then she hands me the paper bag like a kid giving her first present. Well, I reach in, kind of cautious, not knowing what it could be, and what I pull out is an oregano plant. Growing full and already tall, the small round leaves quickly beginning to leak their smell into the kitchen. I sure am surprised, and there is Diane beaming at my thank you and explaining it's from her own garden, that she took my advice and discovered oregano like it was some new fancy spice. She leaves, reminding me to make sure it gets plenty of sun.

I look around. It has been a long time since I've had plants around the house. Now, where was I going to put this one? My eye settles on the kitchen window, the one in the corner where the sun comes streaming in from the deck. I put it down on the sill, and right away the leaves catch the light. Yes, I think, it will grow here.

He Had Dreamed of Returning

For twenty years, Hani had imagined his landing back on the land that had given him birth. He saw himself walking the streets with his head held high and his broad shoulders embracing the world that rightfully belonged to him. People would call him Pasha and Ustaz, and he would find the place he had lost. He was fifteen years old when it was taken away, a young boy on the brink of manhood. He had just started to feel the stubble on his chin, had just begun to think of the girl in the upstairs apartment whose hips swayed as she walked, mesmerizing his vision. It was as if he had stepped backstage and caught a glimpse of the inner workings of the adult world. But before he could follow the ropes and wires to see where they led, before he could look closely at the set to see how it was made, he had been pushed away and the door had firmly closed.

He readjusted his ears to hear what the travel agent was saying on the phone. "Yes, yes," he answered, "these are one-way tickets, I'm sure. Two tickets, one way to Egypt." He was returning at last. Now he was thirty-five years old, a grown man. Yet sometimes when he caught his image passing a store window, he saw only the fifteen-year-old boy he had left behind. It made his steps falter and his voice hesitate; he lost his balance as the world seemed to tilt, shifting time.

Life had been ordinary until 1967. There was school, his friends, his older brother, Bashir, who was in his last year of high school, preparing to take final exams and hoping to get into medical school. But Hani was still in his first year of high school with little pressure and enough time to hang out with friends. He was learning to play the oud, and his fingertips turned hard with calluses as he practiced the chords. His family lived in Maadi, a growing suburb, about twenty minutes from the center of Cairo. The wide streets were tree-lined, and in the evenings they were filled with children on their bikes. Hani would stroll with his friends to a small park where they sat under the shade of trees. Secluded, they would pass around the cigarettes and spend the evening smoking, their talk drifting from political arguments about Abd el-Nasser's regime to the girls they glimpsed at the Cairo American school.

It was one evening when he returned home that he found his family gathered in the living room, his father's face set in grim stone and his mother's eyes puffed with tears. His brother sat in the corner chair, his slender body almost disappearing within the cushions.

"Your brother has been drafted," his father said without turning to look at Hani.

"Aren't they going to wait till he finishes college?" Hani asked. His voice intruded into the room, the words creaking and scraping like an old door caught in the wind.

"You're only allowed a deferment once you're enrolled in college; otherwise they can call you to your military duty whenever they feel like it." His brother spoke from the chair as if he had been rehearsing a speech that now droned in his head.

The days that followed were filled with phone calls and visits, all in an attempt to get his brother a deferment until after college. It soon became clear that he was not the only one who had been called to military duty. The government had sent numerous letters to young men in their last year of high school. Nothing could be done.

On the morning of June 5, 1967, the country woke up to the sound of a battle cry. Overnight, Israel had attacked Egypt and the fight was raging. Radio announcers, their voices hoarse like dried *loofahs*, predicted a glorious victory for Egypt. Parents sat around the radio, sleep crusted on their faces, forgetting the children that scrambled about their feet. It was at that moment that Hani felt himself disappearing, his body retreating into the shadow of itself. He wished he had been the one drafted, that he was out there holding a gun, camouflaged in the desert. But he was here next to his parents who heard each piece of news as if they were swallowing a pebble.

The curfew and mandatory lights out kept everyone indoors in the evening. They sat in the darkness, a pitch-black dark that the town crier called for each night as he walked the streets, bellowing. It was meant to deter the pilots, to give the illusion that they were flying over empty land, not a city filled with the homes of the enemy. Hani sat with his parents each evening until the sounds of the planes flying overhead subsided enough that they could sleep. No one spoke Bashir's name.

When the ordeal ended six days later and the news of Egypt's defeat began to leak through the newscaster's voices, the country groaned like an animal caught in a trap. They had lost their pride and their faith in Abd el-Nasser. And they had lost the Sinai. Hani remembered going there once with his family, watching a bright orange sun rising over the Red Sea, its reds and yellows spread across the water. He swam in the water, and just a few steps from the shore he could look beneath the surface and see corals that astounded his eyes with their colors and shapes, recalling an ancient world.

News of the dead crept slowly into each home until it seemed clear that no family would be immune. Hani's family waited, each knock on the door and each ring of the phone startling them into a paralysis that made it difficult to get up and respond. The news came on a quiet afternoon with a hand-delivered telegram. By then, the news had been so anticipated that it was met with no sound. The three of them walked around the house, weaving a shroud of silence. Even those who came to give their condolences found themselves pulled into it, and they sat with the family for several hours, murmuring only a few words. Bashir's body was returned and the funeral was held. For Hani it was a blur of shadow and movement as people came and went from the house, as he carried a corner of his brother's weight, balancing the coffin with three of his cousins.

The months that followed passed in slow motion. Hani would listen for his parents' voices at night, thinking he would hear them talking about Bashir, but he heard nothing more than the customary good night and its response. His parents seemed unaware of his presence and let him do what he liked. They didn't ask about his schoolwork or question him about where he was going. He began to feel like a ghost as the silence grew around him. It wasn't until almost a year later that he began noticing his parents looking at him with an extended gaze and again addressing him by name. Now he could hear their murmuring at night, but it was his name that he caught being repeated.

"We have to leave, Hani," his father said one evening as they ate dinner.

Hani looked up at his father. His face looked ragged and worn. "What do you mean?" Hani asked, forcing himself to swallow the bite of food in his mouth.

"There's talk of another war, of young men being drafted again," his father said, his chest heaving with the words as if their weight was too heavy for him to utter.

"I don't understand," Hani said.

"We don't want to lose you," his mother responded quickly as if she feared saying the words aloud.

"But where can we go?" Hani asked, shifting his eyes from his mother back to his father.

His father looked firmly at his plate as if the answer were in the rice and eggplant he was eating. "We've been accepted for immigration. We're going to America."

When he looked back on it, Hani could remember nothing between that conversation and the day he found himself standing in the airport with his parents, their belongings tightly packed in six suitcases. They were not the only ones who sought to emigrate. After the war, many families looked around them and saw the end of hope. They opted to leave, to start over again in a country that enticed with its possibilities.

Hani and his family went to Los Angeles, where there was a distant uncle. They stayed with him for two weeks until Hani's father found a job, and they rented a small two-bedroom apartment.

When Hani asked his father about his job, he only said, "Work is work. You go to school and learn."

After being tested, the high school put Hani back a year and placed him in remedial classes. He learned the new vocabulary for science, untangled the sentence structure of English, and memorized the history facts he was given. Only math made some sense; numbers could translate across languages and their sum remained the same. After a year, he was out of the remedial classes and placed in advanced math. But he knew what others saw when they looked at him: a short, frizzy-haired kid who spoke with an accent. He retreated into studying and spent three years of school without making a single friend or attending any social functions.

His teachers saw a hard-working student and encouraged him to go to college. His parents agreed but insisted he had to live at home. They remained in the small two-bedroom apartment so they could pay the tuition. In college, Hani began to see the lines that delineated his world. He could recognize the boundaries that had seemed so elusive to him in high school, the way people created their identities and shaped themselves into who they wanted to become. In Egypt, you were grounded on the foundation of your family, but here his classmates built themselves out of thin air with nothing to attach them to their origins. The haze lifted, and he understood where he was.

His one refuge was still math, and he declared accounting as his major. He enjoyed the accuracy of the numbers on the page, the way they multiplied and divided in consistent patterns. There was no room for deviation. He wrote neat rows of numbers, added and subtracted till his credit and debit columns were balanced.

In his last year, he met Nancy, a senior majoring in education. She was the one who approached him, suggesting they go out for coffee after their statistics class. She leaned toward him as they sat at the small table. She had an easy smile that made Hani want to keep looking at her face. Her smooth skin and blue eyes were framed by light brown hair that curled slightly below her shoulders. Hani found himself unexpectedly doing most of the talking, relaying things from his past that he presumed he had forgotten.

When he graduated and found a job at a small accounting firm, Hani missed the constant activity of college. Nancy was the only person whom he had gotten to know beyond the usual small talk, and he found himself calling her, occasionally going to a movie or dinner. It was a slow relationship. He caught himself by surprise one day when he asked her to marry him. When she laughed and said of course, he felt like he had just scored high marks on a test.

"There is just one thing," he added, taking a step back from her kiss.

"What?" she said, her eyebrows furrowing into a rare puzzled expression.

"Someday, I might want to go back to Egypt. I don't mean just to visit. I want to live there. Are you willing to do that?" he asked.

Her face reverted to its smooth texture. "Of course," she said, "It would be wonderful."

Her answer surprised him. He had expected she would resist the idea, would say she was only willing to visit, but Nancy accepted the possibility with the same ease as when she had first asked him out for coffee.

They sold the house and most of their belongings. Hani didn't want to put anything in storage, and Nancy didn't complain. "This is a one-way trip," he said. "What's the use of leaving things behind? We'll buy what we need there. We'll build a new home." But it wasn't a new home in his mind; rather, he almost expected to find a home there with his name written on it, as if the world had stood still waiting for him. He pushed aside his apprehensions firmly. He was going home. And through his cousin, Amir, he had managed to secure a job at a good accounting firm. Yet, Nancy's open enthusiasm perturbed him.

"Aren't you worried," he asked, "about how different it will be, and you don't know the language?"

"No," she said, "I'm not worried at all."

He tried to take some refuge in her open embrace of their new future.

The plane landed with a series of bumps on the runway until it finally settled onto the smooth ground, speeding toward the gate. He had held Nancy's hand as the plane made its descent; when it finally stopped and he let go, he was surprised to feel the sweat coating his palm. There was no use trying to get up and retrieve their carry-on bags. The other passengers had risen out of their seats well before the seat-belt sign had gone off, pulling bags from under the chairs and suitcases from the overhead compartments. Now the aisles were jam-packed with limbs and bundles. Hani and Nancy trailed the line saying thank you to the stewardess, whose face looked worn and tired.

In the airport, Hani caught the first whiff of Egyptian air, and his nostrils flared as he inhaled the mixture of dust and sweat. The passengers split into two lines, one for those holding Egyptian passports and another for those holding American ones. He and Nancy divided their belongings and separated. Hani wanted to enter with his Egyptian passport, to officially reclaim his identity. Nancy turned to smile at him as her line moved more quickly toward the glass cubicle. Hani waved back. He had placed his handbag on the floor and was pushing it forward with his foot as the line slowly trespassed toward its destination. He watched Nancy approach the passport security cubicle. He saw her hand her passport to the man. Even from this distance, he could see the glimmer in her eyes as she smiled. Her passport was stamped, and she stepped beyond the line. Slowly, Hani approached the cubicle on his side. Eventually he was close enough to catch some of the words being passed back and forth between the officer and the passengers as they stepped up to their turn.

The words slid through their lips, an intonation of guttural rhythms that Hani's ear had to chase and try to corner into meaning. He knew what the words meant, but the tones and gestures rang distant to him. When his turn came, he handed the officer his Egyptian passport, sliding it under the glass in silence. The officer, his mustache masking the youth of his face, opened the passport and glanced at his vital information before looking up to hold Hani in his gaze. The officer's eyes were like a camera clicking his photograph, catching his image from every angle.

"You've been gone a long time," the officer said as if he were noting the random time on the face of a clock.

"Yes," replied Hani, finding nothing else to add.

"Why are you back?" the officer asked. His tone carried an accusation that made Hani twist his body.

"I . . . I wanted to return to my country," Hani said, but the words sounded crooked to his ears, as if he had used the wrong verb tense.

"Is this your country or the great America? Haven't you forgotten us?" The officer's dark eyes pierced Hani as he spoke.

Hani felt his breath held inside him like a balloon blown too big.

He wanted to declare that the officer should simply do his job and stamp his passport, that he had no right to ask these questions. But he only said, "I wanted to come home," knowing that his voice sounded like he was again the fifteen-year-old boy who had stepped through these gates to leave.

The officer stamped his passport and slid it back to him with the welcome greeting, *"Ahlan wa sahlan."*

"Shoukran," Hani muttered softly in thanks as he took his passport and walked away from the booth.

Nancy's tap on his shoulder surprised him, having almost forgotten she was there. "What took so long?" she asked.

"Just bureaucracy," he muttered. "Let's go."

The apartment his cousin had found for them was quite spacious, a top-floor flat in an eight-story building. The balcony off the living room overlooked Taha Hussein Street and provided a view of the island of Zamalek. Buildings rose and fell, creating an uneven skyline. Hani could see a bright neon sign in the distance on top of one of the buildings, displaying the red letters of Coca-Cola in English. There was another small balcony off the bedroom. It sat parallel to a balcony on the building next to them. Only a space of maybe five or six feet separated them. Looking out made him feel watched, and he stepped back into the room.

"It's wonderful," said Nancy to his cousin, Amir.

"I'm glad you like it," replied Amir.

"Yes, thank you," said Hani, realizing he had not done the proper thing quickly enough and thanked his cousin.

"You're tired now," said Amir. "Get some sleep, and I'll come back tomorrow afternoon."

Hani woke to the sound of cars honking furiously and a man yelling out *Ahmed,* his voice ricocheting off the buildings till it vibrated inside Hani's head. He looked over at Nancy; she was sound asleep. He pulled the blanket onto her shoulders and got up. Looking out the window, he saw the jigsaw of morning traffic. Black and white taxis dotted the streets, and a myriad of children in school uniforms, some of them looking no older than four or five, zigzagged their way through the moving pattern of cars, their bodies missing them by inches. Hani rubbed his eyes as if he could change the scene in front of him.

He walked into the kitchen to make himself a cup of coffee. Hs cousin had bought them a few basic items, and he found a jar of Nescafe in the cabinet. He settled his body in one of the kitchen chairs, but after a few moments, he began to shift his posture as the wooden slats pressed into his back and the small seat felt inadequate. Carrying his cup of coffee, he walked to the living room and sat on the couch. The cushions were soft and he felt sunk in. With one gulp, he drank the rest of the coffee and decided to take a shower. By the time he got out, he could hear Nancy in the kitchen and smell scrambled eggs cooking.

His cousin arrived in the late afternoon to take them to see the rest of the family. As the door to his uncle's house opened, Hani found himself caught in the strong embrace of his aunt, his face cupped in her hands in a gesture he had not felt for twenty years. She kissed him on one cheek, then the other, then again, back and forth, till he lost count. From one relative to the next, he felt his body shuffled through the room, enfolded by aunts and uncles and cousins whose faces he perceived through a fog. There was food and laughter and questions. Hani found himself at center stage, his eyes blinking at the brightness directed at him. His ears picked up only a rush of sounds, unable to distinguish voices and words. He would begin to answer someone's question, but halfway through his slow answer, another question would be thrown at him, and he would interrupt himself to answer that one.

Only a few familiar eyes and smiles caught him as he glanced at the panorama of faces in front of him. In the middle of this apartment, he suddenly saw his absence of twenty years open like a cavern. The aunts and uncles of his parents' generation had aged and now looked like the grandparents he had left behind, who were no longer here. And there were young men and women in their teens and twenties that circled the family, sitting on the arms of chairs and sofas, mingling on the fringes. They had been children when he left or not even born; now they looked the way he had imagined himself before he left.

Hani darted his eyes around the room, searching for Nancy, and finally saw her sitting on a couch between his two great-aunts. She held a plate of food on her lap. With each bite, his aunts explained to her what she was eating and how it was made. Nancy looked comfortable sitting in the middle, and she seemed to balance the plate and the conversation with ease.

The days that followed were filled with more family visits. The Arabic began to run smoothly over his tongue, but Hani found himself less inclined to talk and resorted to giving formulaic answers to his relatives' questions. No one spoke Bashir's name. He waited to hear someone mention him or to at least talk of the war, but it seemed to have been erased from the daily fabric of their lives. Nasser had died then Sadat had taken over. The '73 war had restored some of Egypt's pride, and the peace agreement of '78 had given them back the Sinai, only to be followed by Sadat's assassination. Now Mubarek had been president for almost eight years. In America, Hani and his parents had watched the news in their small living room then continued with their lives the next morning.

Two weeks after their arrival, Hani woke up to start his first day of work. He had been assured that he could have more time, allow himself to get settled and adjust to the time difference. But he was eager to begin work, to establish a routine for his days. He had missed the feel of numbers at his fingertips.

Getting ready that morning, he heard a man blaring his voice, yelling out *rubikya.* His hands faltered as he knotted his tie, remembering the cry of men pushing their carts on the streets, asking for old things to buy that they would turn around and resell to others. It was an old memory that had slipped away over the years.

As he made his way through the early morning streets, he had to compete with others who were rushing to work and school. He caught a taxi and gave the driver the address of the accounting firm in the suburb of Mohandessein.

Wiping his sweaty palms, he entered the office. His nervousness subsided as he was greeted with warm smiles. The day passed quickly with introductions and explanations. Yet he sensed an odd distance from his new colleagues. From some, he felt an exaggerated respect as if he held some prize that others could only stare at in awe. From others, there almost seemed to be a tone of ridicule as if he lacked the capacity to perform a simple task.

His days fell into a routine, and he held onto the consistent pattern to keep himself steady. Slowly, he began to earn a certain respect from his coworkers as they recognized his ability to do his work efficiently. But at times, he would step out of his office to realize that he was the only one working and everyone else was socializing. He would quickly retreat behind the closed door of his office.

Nancy had busied herself with setting up their apartment and had quickly been taken in by the older women in his family, who were teaching her how to cook Egyptian food and how to navigate her domestic duties. Hani was surprised at how quickly she learned enough Arabic to enable her to do the grocery shopping and even negotiate with the storekeepers so they didn't take advantage of her foreignness to overcharge her. He was still being asked by strangers where he was from, and when he said he was Egyptian, he was met with an expression of suspicion that made him feel like a child telling a lie.

Once Nancy seemed to have mastered her new duties, she began to look for a job and quickly found one at a nearby

English-language school, teaching fourth graders. Hani assured her she didn't have to work, but her enthusiasm was clear. She slipped into her new position easily and came home with stories of the children's behavior and small gifts that they gave her. She seemed to have established easy friendships with the other teachers and relayed to Hani the intrigues they shared with her. Hani listened but found he had nothing to offer. His days at the office were quiet, filled only with the columns of numbers.

At his desk, Hani's mind sometimes wandered from the work in front of him. Was this what he had imagined? He went to work and returned home every day, but the rest was empty space. Occasionally, they were invited to dinner at one of his cousins' or uncles' houses. Yet as the evening stretched, he became edgy. The conversation would turn to people he didn't know, events he had not been there for, or politics he didn't fully grasp. Nancy would be in the kitchen with the other women, and he could hear their humming voices and soft laughter.

A knock at his office door startled him out of his reverie.

"Come in," he said, coughing the dryness out of his throat.

His boss entered, carrying a folder from a project Hani had recently completed. Sitting down, he asked almost casually, "How are you, Hani?"

"I'm fine, thank you," answered Hani.

"Are you enjoying being back in your home country?" added his boss, as if Hani hadn't answered the first question correctly.

"Yes, of course," Hani said, then paused but found nothing else he could add.

"This project you worked on," his boss said, laying the folder open on the desk between them, "is for a very special company and perhaps it needs some explanation."

Hani looked over and recalled that this account had been particularly difficult to untangle, and he had discovered that the company had made several large-sum mistakes. He had put in the corrections and written a report, showing that the company had failed to reveal its full earnings for the year.

"Yes," Hani said, "I wrote a report explaining what I found."

"Yes, this account really should have been given to someone else, but since it was mistakenly given to you, let me explain. Hani, you haven't been back long, and you left when you were still a child. Egypt is not America. In your America, everything can be precise but here sometimes we need to help our customers."

"But I did everything correctly," Hani began defending himself. "This company said they had a deficit last year but their earnings were significant."

"Here, Hani, look, this is a very special company, and they're very generous in what they pay us. I re-did the account and certainly, you can see that they did have a deficit."

He pulled out the forms and made his way down each column, giving an explanation that made the numbers blur in front of Hani until it seemed they began to lift off the page and dance in front of his eyes.

"Now, as you can see, this is really very simple," his boss said with a wide smile, "and you just need to sign right here since you were assigned to this case." He held out the pen on his open palm to Hani. Hani looked down at the numbers that had settled on the page in an unrecognizable pattern.

"You just need to sign," repeated his boss. "You're in Egypt now."

Hani took the pen and let his hand sign his name.

"Excellent," said his boss, gathering the folder of papers. "We're glad to have you with us, Hani, and keep the pen, a small gift from me."

Hani left work that day, his brain numb and empty as if all his thoughts had been erased. He rejected the glances of hopeful taxi drivers and kept walking. Crossing the bridge to Zamalek, he hesitated and let his eyes drift across the Nile stretching on both sides. It was beautiful, the water meeting the horizon, with the taller buildings like the Meridian and the Sheraton hotels marking the skyline. But he also knew the Nile had become severely polluted and carried parasites that could kill you.

He kept moving, the water having released the numbness, and now he found his mind retrieving snapshots from memories he thought were too far away to recall. His dad sitting next to the radio, his head nodding to the newscaster's report, and his voice calling out to his mother each success by the Egyptian army that was being announced. "They say there is no doubt, no doubt, we're going to win this war, and soon, and Bashir will be home," he repeated.

Hani twisted through the maze of Zamalek streets, trying to avoid colliding with those eagerly pushing their carts of peanuts and candy toward the children clamoring out of the schools. His father had been transfixed next to the radio, like the rest of the nation, listening, their ears straining to catch each hopeful prediction. And they had believed what they were told, believed every word until the illusion cracked, and there was no victory and no one returning home. The news had been a sleight-of-hand trick, but it had failed in the end, revealing a truth that held no beauty or magic.

Not paying attention, Hani found himself sucked into a group of children who had suddenly spilled onto the street. He lost his direction and was pulled into their throng until at last they dispersed, and he stood alone in the middle of the street, startled when a driver slammed his brakes and honked, yelling at him to move out of the way.

When he entered the apartment, he heard Nancy in the kitchen humming to a song by Amr Diab on the radio. She greeted him with an almost guilty smile when he walked in and turned down the music.

"How was your day?" she asked.

"Fine," he responded, taking off his jacket.

"I'm making stuffed cabbage for dinner. Your aunt showed me how to do it. Is that OK?"

"That's fine," he said.

Over the next few weeks, Hani found himself maneuvering numbers across columns till their placement seemed to be based on the whim of some unforeseen force. He was taught how to begin with the desired total and work his way back up to create the numbers that would lead him there. It was a jigsaw puzzle, but he could cut the pieces in any shape and place them in the order that would create the image that had been requested. In the middle of the night, he would wake up in a sweat, shaking, and when Nancy asked what he was dreaming, he could only say, "I can't remember . . . can't remember . . . how much is five times four." Then he would fall back asleep into a landscape where the ocean's waves washed up numbers, throwing them on the shore like dead bodies.

He went through the motions of each day, but he was floundering, feeling like a fish trying to avoid the snare of a hook. He began to tug at the memories of his life in America, recalling his small apartment, his weekly trips to the supermarket where he bought what he needed and no one asked about his welfare. The anonymity of his life there became a warm cloak he wrapped around himself as he made his way through the maze of streets. He remembered his simple accounting job that he had felt was tedious and found some comfort in the memory of clear columns where each number had its precise place.

That Friday morning, he woke with an awareness that filled his body. As Nancy made the coffee and began cooking breakfast, he watched her slender form move through the kitchen with an ease that he knew he would never master. She placed two cups of coffee on the table and sat across from him.

Perhaps it was better to say it before he took even his first sip, before he allowed another day to begin.

"Nancy, I think we should go back," he said, feeling the words fill the air in the room.

Nancy slipped her tongue between her lips from the first sip of hot coffee. "What do you mean?" she asked.

"I mean, go back to America, to our life there, it was better," he said, his voice growing less confident with each phrase.

"But this has always been your dream, to return home, this is what you told me, this is what you promised me when we got married." Her voice wrapped around the words as if to keep them close.

"It hasn't worked out." He attempted an explanation. "This is not what I imagined. I . . . I think my life is in America."

"But we've only been here less than a year, and I'm happy here." Her voice rose with its own awareness. "I like my job, I feel needed here, I am doing something that matters. And I have friends and your family is so wonderful." She took a breath from her escalating list. "I don't want to leave."

Hani looked at Nancy. He knew she had settled into this place as if it was always meant to be her home. "I can't stay," he said feebly.

He didn't go back to the office, didn't bother to collect anything there he might have left behind. And he announced his departure to his family over the phone, so no one could see him, so he would not be forced into finding answers for their questions. Only his cousin Amir came over to drive him to the airport just as he had brought him. He didn't ask any questions, only wished him the best of luck with a sincerity that scratched at Hani's stomach. He asked Nancy not to come to the airport, and they said goodbye with a formality that already marked their distance.

His cousin went as far as he could with him inside the airport, until he was sure that he would encounter no obstacles. As his American passport was stamped, the officer caught his eye. "Are you leaving so soon?" he asked with a slight smirk. Hani retrieved his passport without a response.

Finding the correct gate, he waited until finally it was time to go. He boarded the plane, took his window seat and watched as the landscape of desert, water, buildings, and a multitude of people slipped beneath him.

THE SILENCE OF MEMORY

Phone Call Four

Aloo—Aloo—mama ezayek mama how are you—yes, we are all fine—are you well—yes, the new house is nice and we bought furniture—and we also have a garden—no, there are no fruit trees but the flowers are pretty—tell me was the wedding beautiful—and what did my sister's dress look like—and is he a good man—I wish we could have come but it's hard now because of the new house—and they're going to live with you—yes, we're going to begin the immigration paperwork and hopefully we will be able to bring them—maybe a year or a little more—tell them to be patient and we will do everything—hopefully things will go smoothly and they will come soon—I miss you mama—now it's noon here—it's six o'clock there—tell them we said hello mama and tell them we said *mabruk* congratulations—*ma elsalama ya mama* goodbye mama

Sketches

She struggled with her suitcases, two large ones that had no wheels and a smaller one with a handle. She tucked the handle of the small one into the crook of her elbow so it would be coaxed along with less effort then lifted the other ones. She felt pulled down, the gravity weighing her closer to the ground, threatening to trip her into a heap with suitcases piled on top of her contorted body.

It was two o'clock in the afternoon. The sun seemed to have hit its peak and extended its heat directly above her. She felt a trickle of sweat begin to slide alongside her nose, but she couldn't stretch either arm enough to wipe it off, so it slid further to the corner of her lips where it dissipated. Her shoulder lifted to rub her cheek, slipping her long black hair away from her face. She moved her load a few more steps until she was in front of the office door then stood helplessly trying to figure out how to reach the handle. She let go of the suitcase in her left hand and pulled the door open, pushing her back against it to hold it, then reached down again to pick up the suitcase and moved inside quickly before the door could hit her back.

As soon as she reached the desk, she let all three pieces of luggage drop to the floor. Her hands remained in the same clutching position, and as she unfolded each finger, she could feel the ligaments twist back to their natural shape. The inside of her elbow was red and indented into a crisscross of patterns. She didn't try to stretch her arm out.

It was a small office with a counter, behind it a space that couldn't hold more than one person without some difficulty. A chair had been placed in the corner. It had a black leather seat and a hard wooden back. She suspected that no one had ever sat in it. She cleared her throat and allowed a questioning hello to escape into the empty space behind the counter. The sound of her voice surprised her, and she realized that since she had left the New York airport, she had spoken only a few necessary words.

"Coming," a middle-aged man announced as he emerged from some indeterminate space. He was wiping his hands on a towel as if he had just finished drying some dishes.

She cleared her throat again, fearful that her voice might not be understood otherwise. "I rented an apartment over the phone."

The man slipped the towel beneath the counter and lifted his head to look more directly at her. His gray eyes matched his graying hair. He had on a faded white shirt that had been through the laundry too many times. She had to blink to hold his image, fearing that his body would blend into the space behind the counter. She could feel his gaze on her, and she knew he was taking in her dark eyes and brown skin, assessing her complexion and shape as if trying to calculate the answer to some equation.

"You a student?" he queried.

"Yes." She allowed the answer to slip out, knowing it was the correct one.

"When did you sign the contract?"

"About a month ago, but I paid the deposit over the phone with a credit card."

"What's your name?"

Again she felt his eyes on her, waiting for the right answer.

"Lily Abraham," she said, knowing it was close enough.

"OK," he said with a tone of resignation. "Here," he added, pulling out a few sheets of paper from beneath the counter.

"This is a copy of the lease and the apartment rules. I'll get your keys." He slipped back through the side door and emerged a minute later to hand her the keys.

He watched as she put them into her pocket and then bent her knees to pick up her load, reconfiguring the bags on her arms. She stepped back through the door the same way she had come in.

When she finally entered the apartment, she dropped everything into a heap by the door. She walked through the rooms. Of course it was smaller than she had imagined from the pictures she had seen on their website. As soon as you entered, you were in the living room, a small rectangular space, its only redeeming value was the large window overlooking the woods in the back of the apartment complex. Off the living room was the kitchen, clearly sized to accommodate only one person. Another door led to the bedroom, a square room with a bed, dresser and night table set up in it. And there was the tiny bathroom. All the space had been efficiently used, leaving no unnecessary nook or cranny. It was a space meant to be inhabited, not lived in, a place that you forgot the minute you moved away from it.

"At least it's furnished," she said aloud as she sat down on the couch in the living room. But as she looked around, taking in the sparseness and angular lines that intersected at various corners, she knew that she liked it. She liked the fact that everything was accounted for, that nothing was extravagant; nothing made this apartment distinctive. Anyone could live here.

She began to unpack, placing her things carefully in drawers and closets, so the apartment looked essentially the same when she was done. In the bottom drawer of the dresser, she put a packet of papers and photos bound with two rubber bands without glancing at them. She had taken everything that she might not be able to return for.

When she had rifled through her drawers at home to pick

through the pictures, school reports, and all the papers accumulated in her twenty-three years, she knew she had to make careful choices. She had sat on the floor in front of her desk, the bottom drawer open, where she kept the odds and ends: a journal from high school, a picture of her college graduation, a report on the Pyramids she had done in fourth grade. She took the few things that still felt important; the rest she threw out. She kept the journal and the picture, the report she discarded.

Now, as she sat in the chair by the living room window, looking out on the woods filled with pine trees, she took stock of her position. Her name was Lily Abraham and she was a student, but not really. She was Layla Ibrahim, and she had moved to this Midwestern town with no purpose, neither an acceptance to the large university that dominated the area nor a job, just this apartment designed as carefully as she had fabricated her name. "Maybe I can become Lily Abraham, the student," she said, directing her voice to the trees outside.

When she was a child, she had cringed when her teachers called her name in class. Sensing the hesitation in their voices, she knew her name was next on the roll. They would sound out the letters like a first grader reading phonetically, unable to pull the sounds together to create coherent meaning. "La-ai-la," they would say, or "Laay/la" or "Lee/la," or sometimes, after the "Lay," their voices would halt and they would look up as helpless as a deer caught in headlights. She would have to say the name, her voice combining the letters into a single musical note; then she would slide back into her seat so the eyes staring at her could turn away. Even "Ibrahim" caused problems, the *I* creating an awkward beginning so the rest of the word couldn't follow naturally.

In third grade, a girl had asked her name during recess. While other girls played on the jungle gym and fought over swings, she had been sitting on a bench when the girl came up to her and asked.

"Layla," she replied.

Furrowing her eyebrows into a quizzical look, the girl said, "Kind of like Lily? My sister has an imaginary friend named Lily. Can I call you that?"

"Sure," she answered, relieved at the possibility of an alternative, and she liked the sound of it. No one mispronounced it. It rolled off their tongues smoothly and quickly, never catching anyone's attention.

When her mother heard her friends calling her Lily, she would ask why they were calling her that name. "That's just how they pronounce Layla in America," she would answer and run off before the conversation could continue. Of course her family and their friends continued to call her Layla. She learned to answer to both, but it always took her a second longer to respond to Lily. She hadn't thought to change Ibrahim until she was on the phone a few months ago making arrangements for the apartment. "Last name, please," the woman had questioned. And she just couldn't bring herself to say Ibrahim, to spell it out, have the woman sound each letter back to her like some half-hearted cheer. "Abraham," she had said and hesitated for a second. The woman didn't ask her to spell it. Her name had often been misspelled Abraham, on junk mail and various documents. Besides, the computer didn't put a squiggly red line under Abraham so she knew it was possible.

"Enough," she announced to herself. It was time to move forward. She got up, put on a light jacket to counter the possibility of a cool evening and headed out. She had looked at a map carefully enough to figure out where the university was so she began walking in that direction. Within two blocks, she was on a main street crowded with stores and restaurants and lots of college students. The energy of the place seeped into her, and she began walking faster. This was nothing like the proper tree-lined suburb her parents lived in or the college she had attended near home. She noted the Chinese restaurant crowded with students, the vegetarian place with a long line, and several used bookstores filled with customers. She had come here on a whim, for once allowing a random event to direct her life.

At the bookstore where she had worked near her parents' home, it was usually women who came in looking for the latest diet book or a new self-help book. One day, a young woman came in, wearing jeans and a T-shirt that announced the name of her university. Her hair was pulled into a sloppy ponytail, and her body exuded an energy she rarely saw in the bookstore customers. The young woman was looking for an anthology by Latina women that had recently come out. Of course they didn't have it, but they began to talk and the young woman told her about the large university she attended in the Midwest where the bookstores were abundant.

Somehow that seemed like enough information.

Now, a thousand miles from her parents' suburb in Connecticut, she stepped into a small grocery store, bought a few items and a newspaper.

The phone was ringing as she stepped back into the apartment. Of course it was her mother.

"Yes, Mom, the flight was fine . . . I was going to call you. I was just getting settled in. . . . No, I haven't gone to the biology department. I just got here. Besides, the university is closed now . . . Yes, I'll go tomorrow . . . Everything is fine . . . Yes, I'll call you tomorrow."

She hung up and plopped down on the couch without putting the groceries away. There is the other lie, she thought. And this one would be more complicated than her new name. She had told her parents that she was coming here to do a master's in biology, that she had been accepted into the program. But she had neither applied nor been accepted. She had never told such a blatant lie. The closest was in college. She majored in biology just like they wanted her to. She just never told them about her minor in art. She sneaked in the classes, and if they noticed, she told them they fulfilled general education requirements. What she never told them were the hours she spent in the art studio, the way she liked to go there in the evenings so she could catch the shifting colors of the evening sky, or the hours she spent drawing the same still life from different perspectives. She never explained how she began to draw figures in movement. The model would hold her body still in front of the class, but she could never capture that stillness. It was the subtle movements that caught her eye, the twitch of the leg, a quick scratch of the nose that the model hoped would go unnoticed. Her professors praised her, encouraged her, but a minor was as far as she could push the limits.

Her parents wanted her to become a scientist, hopefully go to medical school. Art was supposed to be her hobby, so she could draw a dog or a cat to entertain her younger cousins. A career had to provide money and, of course, prestige for the whole family. She knew the only way out of the house was to pursue her parents' goals, or at least pretend to. She had lied, said this was the only program that accepted her, that she would continue with a PhD or even medical school at a university closer to home. Lies were easier than the truth when she was expected to live at home until a suitable husband magically appeared. How could she tell the truth when her parents whispered about those whose daughters took off, deserted their families, became selfish Americans, and the parents were blamed for not raising their children properly.

So here she was in the midst of a layer of lies. "One day at a time," she said, shaking herself off the couch. "Tomorrow, I will look for a job."

She slept more calmly than she had expected, and when she woke up to a sunny day, everything seemed less murky. She dressed neatly, and by nine o'clock, she was walking around the center of town looking for help-wanted signs. It was easier than she had anticipated. The second bookstore she tried was willing to hire her, and she could start the next day. One of their employees had unexpectedly quit, deciding on the spur of the moment to drop out of the graduate program in history and move to California. The bookstore manager was pleased that she could work full time, although somewhat puzzled that she wasn't a student. She stumbled through an answer about taking time off and saving money.

It was a typical college-town bookstore, selling an assortment of both used and new books. In the front of the store was a counter where coffee, tea, and various drinks were sold along with muffins and scones. Two small tables and a worn couch were set up for those who wanted to drink or eat and browse the books. It had a more casual atmosphere than the store where she had worked at home, the books a bit scattered and out of order, which seemed to be part of the appeal. The customers, almost all college students, reminded her of the girl with the ponytail.

As the fall semester began at the university, the whole town settled into a routine. The rhythm of classes structured the day for everyone. It was around three in the afternoon when most classes ended that students began filling the bookstore, many of them settling on the couch and at tables. The manager quickly noticed that she tended to gravitate toward the art books in the back of the store. He began to ask her opinion when someone brought in used art books to sell. One day she overheard one of the other workers talking about the art store. After work, she asked for directions and found her way. Easels and paints crowded the window. The inside was just as packed. She walked the narrow aisles; everything was expensive. Still, she bought a small sketchpad and some drawing pencils.

In the apartment, she sat by the window in the living room, the sketchpad on her lap. There were a few squirrels scrounging for nuts, a robin flew off a tree, and the branches bowed slightly as the wind picked up. She sketched the movements she saw, her eye seeing and her hand translating in complete synchronization. "What's the point?" she said aloud, after her third sketch. She closed the pad. "After all, it is just a hobby."

She began to make friends with the students who worked at the store. Slowly, she started to join them in going out to eat or to a small party. There was a sense of camaraderie among them, and it was easy to join in. Her curly black hair and brown skin were less distinctive here among the varied student population. Still, she knew that her features made people look twice, especially her large eyes and long lashes that were often commented on. When someone asked her where she was from, she tried to say Connecticut, hoping it would suffice. But the raised eyebrow and quizzical look told her it wasn't the answer they were looking for. "Egypt," she relented, "but I was born here," she added quickly to avoid the possibility that they might praise her ability to speak English.

Sometimes when she went to the ATM to withdraw money, she'd stare at her reflection in the dark glass. Her face appeared more like a shadow, the oval shape apparent, but the features were only darker shadings. What would it be like, she thought, to fill in the eyes, nose, and lips differently, to keep the frame and change the details? At night, she sketched one oval face after the next, sometimes with small close-set eyes, sometimes with a thin line for a mouth, a nose that was round, a different configuration of features in each oval. But it was hard to get it right, and the marks erasing each attempt seemed to linger, making the new face look transparent.

Every Sunday, she called her parents. It was the pattern they had fallen into. Her mother wanted information about her science classes, how well she was doing, when she would apply to a school closer to home. Her father asked about the safety of her apartment, told her how to install another lock on the door. She felt a tightening in her chest when she spoke to them, as if her lies were blocking the air, keeping it from reaching her lungs. She knew they cared, wanted the best for her, but each phone call became more difficult till she could feel the dread rising inside her as she dialed the phone.

Living at home while she was going to college wasn't bad. It had been easy to get away, saying she had to go to the library or spend more time in the lab. But after she graduated and all she had was the job in the bookstore, there was no reason not to be at home every night and on weekends. She was expected to join her parents' schedule: quiet evenings at home that focused on making dinner and cleaning up afterwards, church every Sunday, the service not ending until one or two, followed by the social gathering and someone inevitably inviting them over for dinner. But the most difficult was the way everyone greeted her at church, looking at her for an extra minute, assessing her. She was available now, had entered the arena of marriageable young women. The adults who greeted her had sons, nephews, and young men in Egypt who would like to come to America. Twice she had given in and gone out on a date with a young man, one a doctor and the other an engineer. Both had dressed formally, taken her out to dinner at an appropriately nice restaurant. Yet she couldn't remember anything they had said and nothing of her own responses besides smiling and nodding at various intervals in the conversation.

She had dated a bit in college, never telling her parents, had lost her virginity by the end of freshman year and felt a relief to be done with it. There were no serious relationships, but it had been fun to go to a few parties, to feel like a real college student. She made some good friends in college, other girls who were struggling with the same issues: what to major in, how to break away from their parents, and what to do after college. One of them encouraged her to join the literary club, and she was asked to design the cover of the literary magazine and do some illustrations. That's how she met Kristi. She was the editor of the magazine. Through Kristi, she got to know other people, most of them English majors. It was fun to hang out with them, put the magazine together, and watch it come out as a finished product. She spent a lot of time with Kristi, designing and laying out the magazine. They often sat for hours at the coffee shop, chatting, unaware of the time passing. Kristi had always known she wanted to study English, to teach, and maybe to write. She came from a small town in upstate New York, and her parents were more liberal, allowing her to move off campus in her junior year. Kristi lived in a small apartment with the two cats she had adopted. Kristi described how they came running as soon as she walked in the door, and the first thing she had to do was feed them. It seemed so ideal, this solitary existence with cats for company, not having to explain yourself to anyone.

In their senior year, Kristi started dating Mike. Rumor had it that he had turned down Harvard to come there. He was handsome with brown hair that persistently fell over his face, giving him a mischievous look as if he had just done something he shouldn't but knew he would be forgiven. He was the star of the college with a 4.0 GPA and several awards. She had thought that once Kristi started dating him, they would spend less time together, but nothing seemed to really change. They still put the magazine together, went to the movies, and, of course, hung out at the coffee shop.

"Do you like him?" she asked Kristi, who was stirring her cappuccino even though she had put no sugar in it.

"Yes, of course," she answered, looking up as if she were answering an unexpected question on a test.

"What do you like about him?" she persisted, trying to make her voice sound casual as she took a bite of her chocolate cake.

"He's smart, and he's funny. You know, he's applying to PhD programs," Kristi answered, listing his qualifications.

"I thought *you* were going to apply to graduate programs," she said.

"Well, we decided Mike would apply first and then when

he gets accepted, I'll apply at the same place so we can be together," she answered, picking up her napkin and folding it again.

They stayed a little longer at the café that day. Walking back to campus together, Kristi slipped her hand inside hers. Her hand was warm, and it felt comfortable to hold it.

The rest of the semester moved quickly toward graduation and the rush of goodbyes as everyone dispersed. Kristi and Mike moved to Boston where Mike had been accepted to graduate school.

In December, Kristi called to say that she and Mike would be in Connecticut and invited her to a New Year's Eve party. She went, figuring it was a better alternative than attending the party her parents were going to at the church. Kristi and Mike's party was at a friend's house. By the time she arrived, it was already full of people and the noise of celebration. There were several friends from their graduating class, and it was good to catch up. Mike was beaming as he described the graduate school he was attending in Boston. Kristi was quiet as Mike talked.

"What have you been doing, Kristi?" someone asked.

Kristi seemed startled by the question, but turning toward the group, she answered that she was working for a temp agency.

"Kristi is getting to know the real world," Mike added with a laugh.

The party dwindled into drinking and dancing. She and Kristi spent the time reminiscing as the noise and movement swirled around them. She had been drinking more than usual, and she could feel her head become lighter, making her happy and oblivious to the rest of the party.

"I better go to the bathroom," she said to Kristi.

"I'll go with you," Kristi added.

The bathroom door shut out most of the noise, turning it into a rough murmur.

"I think I drank too much," Kristi said as she turned on the light

"Me too," she answered.

Kristi leaned toward her and put her arm around her. Her touch was gentle, and she felt herself swaying closer to Kristi. As if following the steady beat of a song, Kristi leaned in to kiss her. She felt Kristi's lips, the sensation slipping down her spine, like light spreading through her body. She kissed her back then someone knocked on the door, the sound breaking their embrace.

Midnight arrived with hugs and kisses getting passed around. She and Kristi gravitated toward each other, holding hands when they could. A little after midnight, people started to leave.

Back in her parents' home, she laid on her bed, sleep quickly approaching. She could still feel Kristi's touch, the sensation continuing to move through her body. She fell asleep, remembering a girl she knew in fifth grade who had long brown hair that fell below her waist. She would stand behind her in line, touching her hair gently, loving the way the softness felt against her fingertips.

The next day she called Kristi.

"Hello, Kristi? It's me."

"Yes," Kristi's voice sounded tired, as if the word was too heavy on her tongue.

"I just wanted to see how you're doing," she ventured.

"I'm fine," Kristi said with finality.

"I was wondering if we could get together?" she asked.

"I don't think so," Kristi answered as if she were losing patience.

"Why not?" She could feel a lump rising in her throat.

"Mike doesn't think it's a good idea," Kristi said with a clear, rehearsed voice.

"I see."

"I have to go now."

That was the end of the conversation as if nothing had happened, not the way they had touched each other and not their entire friendship. She felt something drain from her, as if she were shedding a layer of skin.

After that, remaining at home became more difficult, her parents' lives closing around her, the routine of their days suffocating. She felt removed, often found herself blinking or shaking her head to remind herself where she was. Finally, she told them that she had been accepted to graduate school, that she was moving, and she packed and left.

Here, by herself, what didn't make sense was far removed, kept at a distance, and life fell into a pattern she could sustain. One week, she took a few days off from work and joined some new friends on a camping trip, something she had never done. They camped right by Lake Erie, and she was astounded at the waves that rose high and pounded against the shore. She didn't know lakes could be so similar to oceans, lacking only the smell and taste of salt.

When she got home, her mother's voice was on the answering machine, asking her to call back. She felt a swirling in her stomach, brushed it off as her usual tension about their phone calls. When she called, her mother said, "Just a minute," before her normal greeting. Then she heard her father's voice, so she knew he must've picked up the other phone.

"Where are you?" her father asked, and she could hear the anger gathering behind his precise words.

"I'm here, in my apartment," she responded, hoping it was the right answer.

"How could you do this to us?" her mother's voice was a mixture of hurt and accusation.

"What are you doing there?" her father questioned.

"What do you mean?" she asked, trying to make the words sound bland, but already the rising flood in her body told her they knew.

"I don't understand why you would lie to us," her mother said. "We've done everything for you, given you everything."

"We trusted you, let you leave home and now this," her father declared.

It was useless, but she still said, "What are you talking about?"

"You didn't answer the phone when we called several times last week so we called the biology department. They said you were not a student there. You are not registered for any classes," her father pronounced each sentence like the ending to a story.

"Is that true?" her mother pleaded.

"Why did you leave if you're not studying?" her father demanded.

"I just needed some time away to figure out what I want to do," she said hesitantly, feeling the inadequacy of her words.

"And you can't do that here?"

"Is that how we raised you?"

"You need to come home," said her father with finality.

"We'll send you the money for the plane ticket," added her mother, offering a gift.

"No," she could hear her words as if she had prepared them a long time ago. "I can't come home right now. I'm staying here."

"Layla, what do you mean you are staying? You have to come home."

"No, Mom, I need to stay here."

"You're not our daughter," and she heard her father's phone hang up.

"Layla, please."

"I can't Mom. I'm happy here."

"Then stay, but don't expect to be able to come back just when you feel like it."

Her mother's phone hung up, and she put down the receiver slowly, her hand shaking.

It was over, out in the open, and she felt the flood drain from her body, making her feel weak. She sat for long time looking out the living room window, allowing herself to breathe slowly, replenishing her body with air.

Her parents didn't call over the next few days, and she knew they wouldn't. A synapse had broken. It was up to her to contact them, and it was easier not to. When their phone calls stopped, she felt released, the grip of her ethnicity finally letting her go. But sometimes her breathing felt shallow, and she would stop in the middle of what she was doing, take a huge gulp of air, and let it surge through her body.

The days continued with the routine of work. The only difference was that one day, as she left the bookstore, she found herself walking toward the art department. It wasn't a conscious decision, yet it seemed impossible to be doing anything else. The secretary handed her the usual information. It was too late to apply to the program next year, the secretary explained, but she could take one class each semester as a special student and apply the following year. One class, she thought as she walked home, I could manage that. On the way back, she bought a poster, one of Van Gogh's self-portraits, to hang up in the apartment whose walls had stayed bare.

Spring was a flurry of activity as the academic year drew to a close with students coming in to sell textbooks and buy their summer reading. When most of them left, the town expanded with their absence and the air felt lighter. She began to take more walks, especially around the campus, discovering the large arboretum with flowers now in full bloom. She climbed the winding steps of the old library, finding nooks and crannies among the bookshelves.

The summer heat settled, bringing more humidity than she had expected and the air felt heavy with it. She took trips out of town with friends, especially back to Lake Erie. She liked the expanse of the lake, the high waves, and the purity of the unsalted water.

When the phone rang that Sunday morning, she assumed it was one of her co-workers, but the voice caught her off guard.

"Hello, is this Lily?"

"Yes, this is Lily."

"It's Kristi."

She had pushed the memory back, tucked it inside a pocket, almost forgetting that it was there.

"Hi, Kristi."

"How are you?" her voice sounded hesitant, trying to phrase the question.

"I'm fine."

The pause dragged between them like a child shuffling his feet.

"So, how do you like this college town?" asked Kristi, raising the beat of her voice.

"It's good—there's lots to do and people are friendly," her voice sounded flat to her, but she was afraid to change its tone.

"I broke up with Mike," Kristi said as if she were repeating a sentence she had memorized.

She felt her body contract. "Why?" she asked, not sure she could get the whole word out.

"It just wasn't working out," Kristi said quickly.

She knew it must be her rehearsed response, but she accepted it. She could feel Kristi take a deep breath before she continued.

"Lily, I got accepted to the graduate program where you are. I'm moving there at the end of the summer."

The words sprayed her like water coming out too high from a fountain, splashing her in the face.

"That's great," she said through a gulp of air.

"Lily, I'm sorry about what happened."

"It's OK," she answered, knowing the apology was enough.

"I was wondering if I could stay with you for a couple of days until I found an apartment." Kristi's voice was cautious, as if she were walking carefully, trying not to trip.

She looked at the stream of sunlight edging through the living room. "Sure," she said, "That would be fine."

"Thanks," Kristi's relieved voice said. "I'll call you back with the details."

"That sounds good," she said, feeling her body expand again.

She hung up and went to sit by the window. The sketch pad was on the table next to the chair. She picked it up, turned to the next blank page, and drew the same oval face. The possibilities were infinite.

Suitors

"Wear that blue dress, the pretty one."

Ruffles around my neck fanning my flushed face. I'm tucked into the middle of the room, accentuating the suitor heavily placed in his chair with mirror-shined black leather shoes, pointed stolid. My eyes glaze his contoured belly, pressing out the creases of his shirt, and his head's singular hairline. "When will you be finished with school?" Dancing our gazes, I am silent, receding into my own till the blue dress sits quietly hollowed out.

"Don't stand in one spot. Socialize."

After church, I'm drinking my coffee from a Styrofoam cup, watching my uncle fiddle with his pocket, untucking the lining to recoup a dime. An outlined shadow through the corner of my eye begins a steady trot. He outstretches his hand, a trophy for my grasp. "My name is Samy Amin. I am a dentist. I came from New Hampshire."

Tempted by the gap between his front teeth, I succumb to an outing by the seashore. A walk of intended romance: pause at the wave's unburdening, kneel at the boulder's jutting edge, and hold hands tenderly at the drowning of an orange sunset.

"Your eyes are a sparkling pool of water, a window to see the world," he whispers across the restaurant's basket of bread.

At the waiter's urging, he suggests we order the same fish and chips . . . then we can share. "It would be romantic," he says.

"He's very eager to meet you."

A man recently arrived requests a visit, states his qualifications. Among them, a degree in engineering, a wealthy family with a farm near Alexandria, a desire for children, and a particular fondness for the sweet pastry, *Om Ali.* Since I don't know how to make the pastry, I reject the offer.

When my Great Aunt hears, she writes to divulge the secrets of the future.

My Dear Niece,

Opportunities do not come every day and one must thank God for them. You are twenty-seven years old and beauty fades after twenty-five. Wrinkles begin and then you do not have so much to attract. Be careful—getting an education—you should not be so stubborn. Every woman wants a husband and think about children. He is a good man, an excellent family. They own an *azeba;* not many people have such land anymore. You will be taken care of. No worries so you can stay at home and read your books that you love. You should not throw away such opportunities. God may not grant you others.

Your Loving Aunt

I imagine myself in a few years, the corners of my eyes drooping, my hair gray, my face grooved with wrinkles growing faster than weeds. I wait for the next suitor.

The Couple

"Makram, come here, I'd like you to meet Gamila, she's Ramsy and Salwa's daughter. Gamila, this is Makram. His family just moved to Boston from Ohio. I think you two are about the same age," she added as if it was an afterthought.

"Hi," Gamila said, stretching out her hand then adding, "You can call me Jean."

Makram shook her hand and said, "Nice to meet you. I go by Mark."

Gamila's aunt mumbled something about beautiful names as she slipped back into the crowd gathering in the reception hall after church.

They stood across from each other without moving as if keeping their balance on a tightrope. The crowd shifted around them, gravitating toward the line for coffee and food.

"What made you move to Boston?" Gamila ventured.

Makram looked up. "My father got transferred," he responded.

"Well, Boston is a nice city. I'm sure you'll like it," she offered. After a slight pause, she went on, "Do you have a job here?"

"Not yet, I just finished my graduate degree at Ohio State," he re-aligned his balance a little and pulled his hands out of his pockets.

Makram was tall but slightly built, his frame slender as if trying to keep himself contained in a limited space. Gamila's gaze drifted toward his dark curly hair and wide eyes with unusually long eyelashes. The combination gave him a somewhat boyish appearance, which he seemed to be trying to subdue by keeping a serious look on his face.

"What did you study?" she asked, taking a deep breath.

"Business, with a concentration in marketing," he answered, lifting his eyes to look more directly at her.

Gamila's face was smooth and open, and her brown eyes had a sparkle that hinted at an adventurous spirit. Her body was gently curved, but she was wearing a loose sweater over her dress as if trying to camouflage her beauty. She ran her hand through her long black hair and looked up at him with a clear sense of expectation.

"What about you?" he quickly said, afraid he'd miss a cue, "Are you working or going to school?"

"I graduated from Boston College a few years ago. My major was communications, but I'm just working as a receptionist for now," she added, her voice falling slightly as if she wished she could offer something better.

The crowd had thinned out, and Gamila felt the tug of her mother at her shoulder.

"Goodbye," he said as she turned to join her family.

The couple walked hand in hand through the mall, maneuvering their way between the other shoppers. As they sidestepped a group of teenagers, the woman turned to look at the man to hear him speak, and when he was done, they both laughed softly, holding each other's gaze. They passed Limited Too, where the teenagers stepped inside, and then passed The Children's Place, where one mother was trying to usher her children out of the store.

The woman walked with small, confident steps that seemed to falter only when someone approached her too closely, and then she would glide away slightly. She wore a loose skirt and top that complimented her figure but kept its details hidden. Her long black hair fanned across her back. The young man walked with a slight bend to lean closer to the woman, which seemed to highlight his awkward slender frame. His face opened in a wide smile when she spoke, and, although he rarely put his arm around her, his body moved closer to hers as if to invite the illusion of an embrace.

"Let's get some ice cream," she half whispered to him.

Their steps turned to the center of the mall and zigzagged around the assortment of tables. They stood in line at the ice cream kiosk, waiting behind an older man and his young daughter. The little girl stepped up to the counter, reached up on her tiptoes, and announced that she wanted a vanilla ice cream cone. As the couple spoke to each other, an older woman juggling shopping bags in both hands slid in front of them and ordered her ice cream, her body shoving them slightly aside. They looked at each other, their eyes widening at the insult, but the woman walked off balancing her ice cream with apparently no awareness of their presence. The man behind the counter muttered "What can I get you" with an obliviousness that made the couple stumble over their requests and possibly choose a flavor different from what they actually wanted.

They made their way to a table, slightly disoriented, and sat down next to each other. The woman's eyes darted around, catching the gaze of people looking at them while the man focused his eyes on her. She turned to hear what he was saying and was pulled into his conversation, only occasionally turning her head to take notice of those around them.

She listened to him, but her eyes drifted to his curly hair and then seemed to settle almost hypnotized on the brown tone of his arm.

"Jean, are you there?" he said, waving his hand in front of her face.

"Hmm, yes, yes," she replied, blinking her eyes several times as if to release something inside them. "Come on, let's go look at the new department store that opened up," she added as she scooped up her uneaten ice cream to throw away.

He followed her quickened pace until they reached the store.

"There must be something really good here," he laughed as he caught up with her.

She slowed and took his arm. They wandered, browsing through the store, one salesperson asking twice if they needed help. The second time, the woman turned her back to the salesperson and answered only with an uncharacteristic toss of her head, leaving the man to say no thank you.

"Mark, come look at this," she called out to him.

He came over and she held up one of several mother of pearl boxes displayed on a red velvet background. The corners of his mouth lifted with a sour smile. She turned the box over, and it was clearly stamped "Made in Egypt."

"Do you remember these? My parents bought a bunch of them every time they went back and gave them as presents," she said.

"Yeah, my parents did the same thing. I think we still have a few left," he added.

"Now here they are and you can buy them for just $15.99," she said, her voice rising.

"Come on," he said, tugging at her sleeve, "after all, this is America where everything is for sale. Let's go."

She put the box down, her hand hesitating as if she was tempted to simply take it.

As they stepped back into the mall, their heads turned simultaneously when they heard a loud yell, "Gamila! Makram!"

They turned away from the direction of the shouting, their bodies shrinking. But it was too late, and a woman with large eyes and a wide mouth approached them to once again repeat their names loudly enough to slow the steps of the shoppers around them, causing them to gaze steadily in the couple's direction.

"How are you two? It's nice to see you together. Are you doing some shopping?" She kept up a steady string of questions and comments, eliciting only nods and shakes of the head from the couple until she concluded with "Tell your parents I said hello."

As she retreated back into the crowd, it was the woman who turned to her partner and urged that they leave. The man nodded, and they made their way to the closest exit.

≈

The church hall filled slowly as the parishioners carried their conversations through the pews and down the stairs. Gamila stood by her mother and aunt, holding a Styrofoam cup of coffee. It had turned a murky brown when she added the powdered milk, and after the first sip, she settled for keeping it in her hand as if to anchor her.

Makram was standing farther away speaking to a friend of his father's. But his eyes drifted in Gamila's direction, settling on her face as if willing her eyes to turn toward him. Gamila slid away from the group and gravitated in Makram's direction. He muttered a hasty response to the other man's last comment and ended the conversation.

Reaching a less crowded corner of the church, their postures seemed to relax. They turned to each other in a gesture that almost curtained off the rest of the crowd, but they still kept the required distance away from each other as they spoke.

"How are you, Jean?"

"Good, and you?"

"Fine."

"It's been cold lately."

"Not so bad."

"Are the winters as cold in Ohio?"

"About the same I guess, but there's more to do here."

"Yes, now there's a big circus coming."

"Have you ever been?"

"Yes, I think when I was young."

"Me too."

"Here comes your aunt," he warned as they heard her heels cracking loudly on the linoleum floor.

"Good to see the two of you," she said, kissing them both.

"Nice to see you too," they both mumbled.

"Never mind, never mind, I didn't mean to disturb you, you keep talking." She patted Gamila on the back and retreated.

Several eyes turned toward them, and Gamila shifted her weight, readjusting her stance against the stares entering her back. Makram held his smile still for a few seconds as if it were painted on his face.

"I'll see you later, Mark," Gamila said, directing her gaze at the floor.

"Yes," he answered, "I'll call you."

≈

"At least we're alone," he said, wrapping his arm around her as they settled on the couch.

"You don't think my aunt will come through the door with a megaphone to announce that we're together, do you?" she answered, her lips hesitating into a smile.

"No, the doors and windows are locked, and she doesn't know where we live," he said, glancing outside as if her apparition could still appear.

"Good," she said, "and your parents are definitely gone for the weekend, right?"

"Yes, they're gone, just relax. We're not in church anymore," he responded.

"OK," she said, leaning toward him.

"Oh, do you want something to drink or eat?" he asked.

"Sure," she nodded.

From the kitchen, he yelled out, "There's some feta cheese, potato chips, and some *termus.*"

"Oh, bring the *termus,* that's my favorite," she answered.

He reappeared with a bowl of the lupine beans and sat down.

"Perfect," she said, "we can pretend we're strolling along the Nile."

Gamila's mother was in the kitchen hugging the phone to her ear as she stirred the vermicelli, waiting for it to turn a light shade of brown. "Yes," she said into the phone, "she seems happy, and they're seeing a lot of each other. We haven't said anything." "I don't know," she continued after a pause, "I'm hoping if we don't say anything maybe she'll like this one." "I hope so," she responded to the person on the other end of the line as she added the rice to the vermicelli and continued stirring. "After all, she is almost twenty-eight, it's not a good situation."

Gamila had entered the house and stood outside the kitchen as her mother's voice wafted toward her. She kept her coat on, muffled in its warmth, and shifted her weight in slow motion as if she were a mime. After a few minutes, she jingled her keys loudly and heard her mother hang up.

"Hey, Jean, JEAN? Do you want to join us? We're going to check out the new bookstore during lunch," Sue asked as she slipped on her jacket.

Jean looked up from her desk. "Sure, I've been wanting to go there. But I need to get some food."

"That's fine. Claire is probably going to want to eat too. I'm trying to stick to my diet. We can stop by that place that has pita wraps," Sue responded as she headed for the door, and Jean hurried to catch up.

A crisp fall wind slapped them as they stepped out of the building and into the hectic Cambridge streets. They chatted about the latest office gossip as they walked. Once in the bright bookstore, Claire wandered off to look for a new novel while Sue headed for the diet section with Jean following.

"Maybe I should try this one," Sue said, holding up a glossy-covered book with an enlarged picture of a strawberry shortcake on it.

"Sue, you look fine," said Jean in an indulgent voice. "Here, come look at this travel book about Paris. Maybe we should take a trip."

"Maybe you should take that trip with Mark," said Sue with a slight wink to her voice. "How is that going anyway?"

"It's going well," answered Jean, her voice retreating a little.

"Did you find what you were looking for?" Sue asked Claire at the checkout.

"Yeah, this book is supposed to be really good," said Claire, showing off a cover that displayed a man and a woman in a steamy embrace. "What about you?" added Claire.

"Yes, I think this new diet book is going to work," said Sue. "Jean, are you getting the Paris book?"

"No," said Jean, "I'm just going to pick up a magazine. Maybe it's not the right time for Paris."

≈

It was late, and the only lights came from the few stores that were still in the process of closing. The couple had gone to see a movie and then wandered through the narrow streets of Harvard Square, stopping to look at the window of a clothing store or browse through a gift shop.

"I'm a bit hungry," he volunteered. "Shall we get something to eat?"

"Sure," she agreed, "although things seem to be closing."

The couple held hands as they made their way to a restaurant whose lights were still glimmering. The restaurant looked small but once they entered, they were faced with a large brightly lit dining area. Only a few people remained, most of them drinking or eating desserts.

"Can I help you?" asked a waiter walking toward them.

"Two for dinner," the man said as he wrapped his arm around the woman.

"We're just about to close," answered the waiter, his eyes revealing his desire to leave the neon lit restaurant.

The woman took a small step backwards but the man leaned in, "We won't be long, and you are still open."

The waiter looked up, allowing his eyes to linger on them for an extra moment. "I'll check with the manager," he said.

The couple watched as he stepped away to talk to another man.

"It's all right, we can go," she said, tugging a little at his sleeve.

"No, I think it will work," he said, bringing her closer with his embrace.

They looked up to see the manager smile in their direction and nod. His voice came to them across the restaurant in a broken whisper, " . . . cute couple, let them come in."

The waiter returned with two menus and ushered them toward a table in the middle of the dining room. They sat down, the woman tucking her body into the table and the man inching his chair closer to her.

"Take your time," the waiter said with a smile squirming on his lips.

"Perhaps we should leave, it's late," the woman urged after the waiter had gone.

"No, it's fine," said the man securely, "Look, there are still people here."

The woman looked up, blinking her eyes against the florescent lights of the restaurant and glancing around at the mostly empty tables. A few of the other diners looked in their direction before returning to their own quiet conversations. The dining room was a large circle with tables set up inside like a merry-go-round. Wide mirrors decorated some of the walls. Across the room, the woman's eyes caught the reflection of her face. She startled, not recognizing her features at first. Her face was a painted canvas of browns, dark shades accented by long black lashes and lips bordering on a hue of purple. Next to her, the man's face reflected in the mirror, his features a variation of her own. Their images blended, dark tones highlighted sharply against the brightness of the room.

"What will you get?" the man asked.

Remembering her menu, she glanced down. "Just some soup, I think."

"That's all you want?" he asked.

"Yes," she answered.

The waiter returned to their table, and she ordered the cream of broccoli soup while he ordered the chimichanga special. The woman edged in her seat as she watched the few remaining customers begin to leave.

By the time their food arrived, they were the only ones left.

"This is good," noted the man as he ate, "do you want to try some?"

"No, thanks. It's getting late," she said.

"It's kind of neat being the only ones here," he suggested.

"Yes, I suppose," she responded, turning her head slightly so she could see the manager and the waiter in the far corner of the restaurant chatting and laughing.

As they finished their meal, the manager came over. "I hope you enjoyed your meal," he said. "Would you like some dessert, our compliments?"

"No, thank you," the woman answered quickly.

The man nodded in agreement, adding that he was full.

They stepped out into the night air, tightening their jackets around them. The streets were emptier as they walked toward the parking garage. The woman's silence seemed to permeate the man and he said little. In the garage, he opened the car door for her, but she hesitated for a moment, her eyes searching the ground as if she had lost something.

Bluebird

That morning she glimpsed a bluebird as it flew by the window. She chased it to the next window to see if it had settled on a tree branch so she could catch full view of it. She suspected a nest nearby but had not been able to find it.

Sonya's Saturday morning ritual was to sit on the couch for several hours by the front window, drinking coffee as her hair dried. It didn't need that long now that she had cut it to her shoulders, an attempt to minimize the gray streaks that were rapidly taking over the black. It hadn't bothered her initially, the few gray hairs like accent marks, but when they multiplied in the front, it became disconcerting to look in the mirror, each time surprised by the indication of aging. Finally, she cut it short, letting it fall in the front to minimize the appearance of white. It framed her face on both sides, making it look elongated, and highlighted her nose to an even sharper angle. The result was that her brown eyes and long lashes, once her most pronounced feature, now seemed sunken. Her body, still slender except for her full hips, kept her youth intact for the time being. At thirty-eight, she mostly felt younger until the realization of thirty-nine and then forty approaching held her illusion in check. There was no sign of the bluebird. She gave up on her quest and began the household chores, occasionally turning her head to the window.

Later, when her husband returned from the hardware store, his arms packed with piles of wood and another sharp-edged tool that looked menacing and unbending, she tried to explain how the bluebird had returned. He nodded and responded with an agitated explanation of his plans for renovating the space in the basement to turn it into a media room, moving the TV there and buying a new state-of-the-art stereo system with surround sound. Sonya smiled approvingly and helped him carry the new purchases downstairs. But she had grown accustomed to these new projects and their end results.

Rick would spend the next few weeks continuously downstairs. Each weekend's plans were cancelled due to his project. She'd hear hammering and the occasional yell after some crashing sound. "It'll be a surprise," he'd answer when she offered to help. Finally, he'd emerge, sawdust covering him like powdered sugar, and invite her to view the final project. She had learned to fabricate her initial response, to express the excitement he anticipated. But it was difficult to identify the change. Often, it seemed like he had done nothing more than paint or perhaps put up a shelf on the wall. The house looked endlessly the same to her, and the renovations he claimed to have made eluded her eye. The first time, when she said she couldn't see the change, he had proceeded to give her a tour of the project, the first being one of the upstairs rooms. "Look," he said, "I put new baseboards and new caulking around the windows, and look, I shaved the closet door so it would close all the way." She tried but felt like one of the advisors in *The Emperor's New Clothes,* with too little wisdom to see the riches described.

He fixed up that upstairs room a month after the abortion, claiming that one day they would have children and the house needed to be ready. But after a year of trying and the first test results, he limited himself to renovating various parts of the basement. The pregnancy had come too quickly, just after they had signed the lease on the house.

"You're pregnant," he said, emphasizing each syllable of the word.

"Yes," she answered, keeping her eyes focused on a dirt spot on the rug.

"Well, what are we going to do?" he announced, bouncing his long body on the couch and reaching his arm as if to embrace one of the back pillows.

Sonya shifted her gaze to another spot. "I don't know," she mumbled. She had expected a warmer response.

"We have to pay a mortgage now, I've got to work overtime, and you said you'd do extra work at home." His lower lip pouted slightly as he spoke, and his blue eyes, normally narrow, widened. She knew the look, one that had initially attracted her to him.

"I guess we just can't," she finally answered.

He ran his fingers through his blond hair and that ended the conversation.

She went alone since he had to work. In the waiting room, there were mostly girls, much younger. She could only notice details: one had a nose-ring, another a purple streak in her hair. One held tight hands with the boy sitting next to her. When the girl was called in, the boy left the waiting room and returned later with a bag of donuts that he proceeded to eat.

Sonya lay down, knees up, legs apart, only the doctor's head visible, his hair black and curly, a glimpse of brown skin. The nurse said she could squeeze her hand. The pain was sharp, scratching her body, chalk against board. She pushed her tongue flat to the roof of her mouth, swallowed back the scream. She took the thirty minutes allowed on the cot, body turned into a semicircle, the cramps snapping against her stomach like a racquetball hitting a wall.

Rick came home late that night, after she was already in bed almost asleep.

"How was it?" he asked, slipping into the covers.

"Fine," and she turned back into sleep.

That night, again and again, she dreamed of a young boy. His hair was blond and smooth like Rick's, but his eyes were round and brown, staring like hers. The boy was maybe four or five. He stood still or turned his head slightly so she could better see him, but he did nothing else. She shook the dream off when she woke up the next morning. But a few days later, on her way home, she walked by a school as kids were being dismissed. They were gathered in front of the building, eager to be given the signal to run. As she looked at them, one boy turned his head to direct his gaze right at her. His hair was blond and his eyes round like her dream. She almost turned to walk to him, to take him, as if he were something she had dropped and needed to retrieve. But the school bell rang, and she continued home quickly.

Over the next two years, both she and Rick were promoted and the mortgage was easier to pay. When they started trying, they expected it would happen right away. With each month, Sonya assumed they had just missed it by a day or two and it would work the next time. After six months, both their energies were depleted, and they avoided discussions of what they would name their child.

It was Sonya who finally gathered the courage to make an appointment with a fertility specialist. Each month, as her period arrived, she would become almost immobile, spending days in bed, eating. She had always assumed she would have children, had wanted to have several, although now she realized her age would make that impossible. In the corner of her top dresser drawer, she kept a small black and white photograph of her great-grandmother. When Sonya was a child, her mother would bring out her secret box of various odds and ends, take out the picture and begin to tell Sonya what she knew between her own memory and the stories she had been told.

Sonya's great-grandmother was the last one to live her entire life in Egypt. She was married at sixteen, had raised eight children, but had given birth to more, perhaps twelve. Some died at childbirth and some as young children. Sonya wondered how you could learn to survive the death of a child as a repeated pattern of your life. She knew little else except that her great-grandmother had been married to a stingy man who watched over the household expenses. But stories had come down about how her great-grandmother had succeeded in outwitting her husband. Each year, as she was the eldest, the women in the family would gather at her house to make the Christmas or Easter cookies, one by one, by hand, the *kahek, ghoraiba,* petit fours. They sat around the table in the kitchen, gathering the dough they had kneaded in their hands, shaping it in the groove of their palm to a circle they could open, stuff it with nuts or dates, then pat flat, decorate with the *monash,* sharp like tweezers. The women talked, laughed their secrets, while in the living room the men debated the current regime. Every once in a while, her husband would come in, demand an account of how much flour, how much butter she had used. "Only one kilo," she would reply, thumb and two fingers held together in a plea for forgiveness. And he believed her, despite the abundance that would appear on his table each year. No one knew how she manipulated her budget, how she fed them all with the illusion of so little.

The doctor did test after test, always assuring Sonya the process would yield results. Her days revolved around doctor's appointments, keeping track of her cycle, measuring, recording. Rick kept himself aloof, his only contribution being, "I hope it works." Each test yielded nothing significant: some minor hormone imbalances, a slight blockage. She followed every lead like a detective, taking the appropriate medication, doing the recommended procedure. Rick was asked to go through a series of tests. Sullenly, he complied, but everything appeared normal, and he retreated back to fixing the storage room in the basement. Finally they were faced with the option of doing in vitro.

"Do you think we should do it?" asked Sonya. She had gone down to the basement and was sitting precariously on a stool while Rick hammered at an old bookcase.

"I don't know. Is it going to work?" he replied through a nail held in his teeth.

"The doctor said the chances were excellent since there isn't actually anything wrong with either of us." She shifted her weight to keep a balance on the stool.

"That's what he said about the inseminations and those didn't work." Rick started hammering in the nails.

"I know, but we have to keep trying."

"Is the insurance going to cover it?"

"I don't think so."

"We can't afford it."

The house grew large after that. There were too many rooms that sat still, unused, except for the kitchen and the bedroom and, for Rick, the media room he had fixed up in the basement, which contained simply a couch and a TV with headphones.

It was a large colonial house, somewhat typical for New England, white with slender columns in the front, giving it a kind of miniature mansion appearance. But the pillars were too thin for its large structure, making it seem like the house would tip over if they were removed. The inside was room after room painted in clean white strokes with straight angled walls. Sharp lines, no nooks or crannies; nothing distracted the eye.

Sonya began buying bird feeders in the hope of catching sight of the bluebird, which she hadn't seen for some time. She hung one by the kitchen window. A few birds came, mostly sparrows and doves. She bought another feeder, this time putting it in the front, and she took extra care in choosing the birdseed to make sure it would attract bluebirds. As she stood by the living room window, she saw a few cardinals, one bird with yellow feathers, but still no bluebird. The bird feeders multiplied and were joined by several birdhouses. Sonya kept watch, filled the bird feeders and peeked into the birdhouses. A variety of birds flocked to the yard, but still no bluebirds.

Sonya began to grow uneasy, agitated. She jumped when a bit of wind blew against the window, her shoulders twitched at every creak in the house, and her left eye began fluttering so much she had to place two fingers on it to keep it still. She tried to remember. Her mother had said something about eyes fluttering and bad omens, but it could also be good, depending on which eye, but each person had to figure it out for themselves. Sonya had paid little attention.

Rick suggested a vacation, but she was reluctant to leave in the summer when there was a good chance of catching sight of the bluebird. She continued watching until one morning when she finally glimpsed it through the window. When she lost sight of it, she stepped out to pursue it. Her search took her through the yard from one tree to the next. She even crawled under the Christmas tree, the one they had planted seven years ago when they first moved into this house, now almost ten feet tall. Branches snapped at her sides as she tried to make her way. The pine needles prickled her knees, and she kept picking up her palms, licking them to cool the sharp sting.

Silences

My mother's silences filled our house. They seeped into the walls and crouched in the corners. If you tripped over the hallway rug, they would be lying in wait. If you opened the top kitchen cabinet and reached back for the hidden package of sugar cookies with sprinkles, they would begin to emerge.

At times, the silences only stayed a day or two, but sometimes they remained for as long as two weeks. By then, we could feel them shudder through our bodies and imagine they accompanied us out of the house. Waiting for the bus to school, I would feel a tap on my shoulder, but when I turned no one was there. My younger sister swore they were in her school desk. She dreaded opening it and instead, carried all her books in her knapsack, permanently hunched over by the weight.

The silences came out of nothing we could see. My mother would wake one morning, and for two or three days or more, she would say nothing. It was as if she had left, taken a bus or train to somewhere we couldn't reach and decided to stay there without us. She did all her usual tasks, but without words. At first, my brother and sister and I thought she was upset with us, that her silence was a punishment for something we had said or done. She looked angry, her eyes narrowing into their corners and her lips set like plaster into a mold. When we asked my father, he'd give us his easy smile, tell us everything would be fine, and pat us on the back like we were coughing.

I remember my mother in the mornings, standing in the kitchen preparing our school lunches. By the time I woke, she was already dressed, her black hair combed, always pulled back into a neat bun. She wore only dresses or skirts and always in solid colors. She was only five feet and two inches, but she seemed tall, her back always straight, every muscle stretched to its full length. Her face was brown and smooth. Even as she got older, it remained that way, no wrinkles marring its surface. She smiled sometimes but never with an open mouth, and her smiles never turned into laughter.

As we set off for school, my mother would order us at times to take our raincoats.

"But, Mom," I would complain, "the sun is out. It's not going to rain."

"Take your raincoat," she would firmly insist.

Arriving at school, my brother, sister, and I would be the only ones carrying raincoats, becoming victim to the stares and mocking of our classmates. But, without a doubt, by afternoon, the sky would darken and it would be pouring. Everyone else would be getting soaked and glaring at us as we tried to look more invisible under our coats. Other mornings, the clouds would be heavy and the moisture thick in the air, but my mother would say, "Leave that umbrella at home. You won't need it." We'd try to argue, but her voice ordered us. And each time, the sun would emerge though the clouds. After a while, we gave up the arguments, accepting that our mother had some insight into the workings of nature, which we would never fathom.

My mother stayed at home, cooking, cleaning, and taking care of all our needs. There were three of us, my older brother, my younger sister, and me in the middle, plus my father. Our beds were made by the time we returned from school, our laundry done and neatly put away. Every night there was dinner on the table. My mother cooked healthy, bland food that sustained our bodies without exciting our taste buds. Once, my brother brought home some hummus that one of his friend's mothers had made. It was spiced with garlic and red peppers that sent sparks down our throats. We devoured it as my mother walked out of the kitchen, warning of upset stomachs. For the next three days, her silence reigned over us.

We knew almost nothing about my mother. My older brother expressed little interest, and my younger sister said she didn't want to know, perhaps fearing the information would weigh her down even more. Once, I asked my mother if she had ever had a job. She raised her eyes to look at me as if I were three years old and had just asked where babies come from then simply said her family and her home were her work. I started to open my mouth to ask again, but her eyes were concentrated on the sewing in her hand. Catching my father alone a few days later, I asked him, but all he could tell me was that she was working as a secretary when he met her. "What kind of a secretary? Did she like her job? Did she have any career goals?" I asked. It was my last year of middle school, and I was beginning to think about what kind of job I wanted to have one day. But my father couldn't say more. He didn't know any of the answers, only that as soon as my brother was born, just a year after they married, she quit her job and stayed at home.

My father was an easygoing man, a plumber who believed you should only fix things if they were broken. Our toilets and sinks always flowed smoothly, but if we complained that there wasn't enough hot water for all our showers, he would simply say, "You can wait till the water warms up or take a cold shower." He was five feet seven, although he often looked shorter than my mother. By the time my brother and I were fifteen, we had both exceeded my parents' heights; only my sister seemed to inherit their genes, ending up just an inch taller than my mother. My father's most prominent feature was his balding head. I don't recall that he ever had a full head of hair. He was a little round in the stomach. Having grown up in a family where there was barely enough for everyone, he ate my mother's bland food with relish.

The little we knew about my mother came from my father. He met her when she was twenty-eight, five years after she had arrived from Egypt by herself in 1968. What had she done for those five years? I asked, but he had no idea. She was never forthcoming with the details, and my father was a man who accepted whatever a person was willing to offer. Over the years of their marriage, he had gathered bits and pieces of her past like scraps of paper you write a note or a phone number on then misplace. When you find it years later, you're unable to recall the relevance of the information. Her brother fought in the 1967 war and never came back. Her family waited and waited after the six days of fighting was over. He never returned, his body was never found, and there was nothing left. Her mother sat and waited, her eyes fixed on what only she could see, her son's figure fading after he kissed her goodbye.

"Did they ever find him?" "Is her mother still alive?" "Does she have any other sisters or brothers?" I asked, breathless from hearing the story. But my father knew nothing else. Once my brother was born, he said, she stopped talking about her past and the silences began.

My brother and sister seemed content with the little my father was able to tell them. But my curiosity persisted. It was ironic since my brother looked the most like my mother, having inherited her black hair and distinct features. Yet he was like our father, willing to accept life as it appeared, never probing beyond the surface. My younger sister seemed to have delved back for her genetic makeup, coming out with red hair and eyes that looked green in certain lights. My father claimed he had a grandmother with the same looks. I looked the most like my father with brown hair and a pale complexion, although my eyes were a firm brown unlike his blue ones.

Every once in a while, I would venture with a question,

hoping my mother would reveal some piece of information that would help me to understand her.

"Mom, what is Egypt like?"

"It's just a country like any country."

"What kind of house did you live in?"

"Just an apartment."

"Did you have any brothers or sisters? Do I have any cousins?"

"Everyone's gone now."

"Can we go to Egypt one day?"

"Go do your homework."

It was useless. My mother's answers buried us in the present.

The dream began when I was about sixteen. I'm in a big field running around with friends, all of us chasing each other. Then four of the kids pick up a big white canopy off the ground, like a parachute, and begin to lift it up so it balloons out. Somehow, I end up standing in the center right under it. They lift it up higher and higher above me then it begins to fall, but just before it reaches my head, they lift it up again. My heart starts beating faster and faster, fearing it will come down on me and suffocate me. Each time, I wake just as it is about to sink over me.

My brother went away to college when I was sixteen. Each year, he came home less and less frequently until he even stopped returning for the summer. When he did come home, I would tell him how mother had grown more silent, how even when I asked her where she got the little duck figurine on her dresser, she'd say she didn't remember. But college seemed to have washed away the last of his curiosity. And he'd say, "It doesn't matter. Just live your life." But I couldn't. As I got older, I asked more questions, prodded her, trying to get some piece of information.

"Mom, are you Muslim or Christian?

"These things don't matter."

"But was your family Muslim or Christian?"

"Good people are good people no matter what religion they believe."

It was no use. Her lips would retreat into a thin closed line.

I went to a college about two hours away. Unlike my brother, I couldn't bring myself to go halfway across the country. I came home for holidays and summers. I stopped asking my mother questions, but I stayed close to her, helped her with the mundane errands, the cooking, making do with her physical closeness. She listened to my college stories with little comment, and every time I announced a new major, whether it was history or dance, she simply said, "That's good. Keep studying."

When I came home the Christmas of my junior year, having finally decided on a major in biology, my mother didn't look well. Her dark eyes had sunk deeper into her face, and her hair looked thin and faded. It seemed harder for her to raise her lips into the dutiful smile she had always given us. My sister wasn't home that year, having decided to go on a study-abroad program in London. When my brother came over, I asked him what he thought, but he insisted that he didn't see any difference in her appearance. I cornered my father until finally he admitted she seemed a little tired, but he felt sure it was because we had all left home and there was less for her to do.

When I came back that summer, I was stunned by her appearance. She seemed to be a gaunt reflection of herself, her bones protruding as the clothes hung on her thin body.

"I decided to go on a diet," she said in answer to the look on my face.

I blinked back the tears that were straining to the surface. "You look great," I forced the words out.

The next day, I convinced my father to make her a doctor's appointment. My mother had always made our check-up appointments on time, but I couldn't recall her ever seeing a doctor. We tricked her into going, saying I had to buy some stuff for school. When she realized we were at the doctor's office, she looked at me like an animal that had been tricked into a trap.

It was cancer, too far gone to do much, the doctor said. We could do some chemotherapy; it might help, he suggested. I thought she would resist, but she retreated into her silence and let my father and I make the decisions. After each chemotherapy session, she looked haggard, like someone who had been climbing a mountain too steep for their strength. After a few sessions, she had to be hospitalized because she became so weak.

I sat with her in the hospital room. She was lying on her back, an IV attached to her right arm. She had become so thin that I could hardly distinguish the outline of her body beneath the covers. I slipped my hand into hers and she turned to look at me, a slight flicker of a smile hovering around her lips.

"Mom, you're going to be fine. The doctor said you can come home in a day or two."

"You've always been a good daughter, the one who stayed close."

"I'm right here, Mom."

"I want you to be happy."

"Mom?" I wanted to ask her a million questions at that moment, to repeat the questions I had asked through the years, but she looked so tired, the effort of her words marked in the quiet of her voice.

I left when she fell asleep, after visiting hours had already ended.

When I finally closed my eyes that night, the dream returned, and each time, the canopy fell lower and lower before the children lifted it back in the air. It came down again and touched the top of my head, its weight much heavier than I imagined. It forced me to my knees as I felt it push my body closer to the ground. I woke up with a scream, the sweat pouring down my face and my body shaking. I sat up breathing heavily, disoriented, until my father came in. He stood next to me as my breath slowed down.

When the phone rang, he went to answer it and I heard his voice.

"Yes, yes."

"I understand."

"Around three o'clock."

"Quietly."

"Yes, no pain."

"Yes, thank you."

I looked at the clock. It was four in the morning. My father and I sat next to each other. We said nothing as slowly the light made its way into the room.

My brother and sister came home, and we made arrangements for the funeral. I waited for a phone call from Egypt, a letter, a telegram, someone unfamiliar who resembled my mother to show up. When nothing came, I began rifling through my mother's things, spent hours looking through books, magazines, papers, but all I found were recipes written neatly on index cards, local phone numbers jotted down in an address book, nothing that would reveal her past or mine. The funeral was small, only us and people who knew my mother from the neighborhood and the schools we attended.

My brother and sister left after a few days, my father assuring them that he would be fine. And I knew he would be. He accepted my mother's death the same way he had accepted her presence, with no questions. All I had were the pieces of stories she had told my father that first year of their marriage and the memory of her silences.

Phone Call Five

Aloo—Aloo—yes mama—how are you—*kol sana we entee tayeba* Merry Christmas—how are you doing—yes, we are all well—my sister and her husband bought a house—yes, it's nice—no, it's not too far away from us—are you well mama—*kol sana we entoo tayebeen* Merry Christmas to all of you—no, we didn't go to church—because we had to work the next day and it's too hard—we celebrated on the twenty-fifth of December this year—because there is a vacation and everyone celebrates—the trees and the lights are beautiful—and where are you going today—mama we want you to come—why mama—think about it—here everything is good—and we can do the paper-work for you—ok mama—no, now it's twelve midnight—the time changed again—it's seven in the morning for you—bye bye *ya* mama

PAULINE KALDAS is an associate professor of English at Hollins University. She was born in Cairo, Egypt, and immigrated to the United States in 1969. She is the author of *Letters from Cairo* and the poetry collection *Egyptian Compass.* She is also co-editor with Khaled Mattawa of *Dinarzad's Children: An Anthology of Arab American Fiction,* now in its second edition, which won the 2005 Silver Award in *ForeWord Magazine*'s Book of the Year. Stories from *The Time between Places* have appeared in a variety of journals and books including *Callaloo, Mizna,* and *Ripe Guava.*